PURE DUMB LUCK

DAHLIA DONOVAN

For information, contact the publisher, Hot Tree Publishing PTY LTD.

www.hottreepublishing.com

Editing: Hot Tree Editing

Cover Designer: BookSmith Design

E-book ISBN-13: 978-1-925853-84-1

Paperback ISBN-13: 978-1-925853-85-8

THE GRASMERE TRILOGY

DEAD IN THE GARDEN

DEAD IN THE POND

DEAD IN THE SHOP

THE SIN BIN SERIES

THE WANDERER

THE CARETAKER

THE BOTANIST

THE ROYAL MARINE

THE UNEXPECTED SANTA

THE LION TAMER

HAKA EVER AFTER

STANDALONES

AFTER THE SCRUM

FORGED IN FLOOD (M/M/M)

FOUND YOU

ONE LAST HEIST

THE MISGUIDED CONFESSION (M/F)

ALL LATHERED UP (free—e-book only) (M/F)

NOT EVEN A MOUSE (free—e-book only) (M/F)

AT WAR WITH A BROKEN HEART (M/M/M)

HERE COMES THE SON

PURE DUMB LUCK

DEDICATION

For Becky, who coerced me into writing the full story.

CHAPTER ONE

WOODY

"Go inside. Buy your lottery tickets. Shoot the shit—all calm and natural-like." Woody gripped the steering wheel of his pickup truck tightly, trying to talk himself into getting out of it. A familiar pep talk. Familiar and oft repeated. "You've known Eddie since elementary school. You've been staring at his ass since he played quarterback to your running back in junior high. No point in getting all fucking weird around him now."

Patting the bobblehead football player on his dashboard for good luck, Woody reluctantly slipped out of his truck. He slammed the door and plastered a grin on his face. Lottery tickets wouldn't buy themselves.

And Eddie had already seen his truck. If he ran away now, he'd never hear the end of it. The temptation to get back into his vehicle was strong.

C'mon.

This is not even close to the hardest part of your day.

Except it had definitely become the most difficult

daily event. Woody had never considered himself a coward, yet every single morning, he walked into the gas station to see his best friend, the person he'd been in love with for years, and said nothing beyond small talk.

He never told the truth of the ache in his heart growing too painful to ignore. He couldn't. What if Eddie rejected him?

"Your usual?"

Woody grinned at Eddie, who ran the family-owned gas station in their little country town nestled in the middle of a national forest in the southern Appalachian Mountains. "You know me. Boring as shit. I'm consistent, at least."

"One large coffee, one pack of powdered donuts, and three lottery tickets. Two for you, one for me." Eddie rolled his dark brown eyes and held out a large hand for the card Woody held out to him. "You never change, dude. You've been doing this for twenty years—since high school. I know Coach said you were full of dumb luck, but I don't think he meant with the Mega Millions."

"Have a little faith, Eddie." He grabbed both his breakfast and the lottery tickets, winking at his oldest friend, who hadn't changed much in the thirty years since they'd known each other. *Still as fucking hot as the day I first saw him in the shower at the gym.* His warm brown skin had glistened under the shower. *Maybe stop thinking about Eddie naked in the middle of the gas station.* "We still on for fishing this weekend?"

"Unless you get lucky with your numbers. If you do, we'll go fishing on a yacht instead of your granddaddy's rickety old boat." He tapped a finger against the ticket stub in Woody's hand. "Go on. Get your ass out of here. You're ruining the atmosphere. Plus, I like watching you leave."

For the past twenty years, they'd danced around each other. Woody had given up on anything happening between them outside of harmless flirting. Maybe it was too clichéd—two former jocks who fell in love on the football field finally getting their chance in their late thirties.

It sounded like a cheesy movie plot.

The only way I'm getting lucky at this point is with the lottery tickets.

And I'm all out of luck with that as well.

I wouldn't mind winning eight million even if taxes take a massive chunk of it.

It had to beat working for his little brother in the construction business. Woody loved JJ, but he was as much of a pain in the ass now as he'd been as a kid. Putting away his dreams of winning, he focused on doing what he'd done since his teens: getting to work.

He scrubbed his fingers tiredly through his graying black hair. He kept it short, though not as close as Eddie, who was a sixteenth of an inch away from being bald. *I'm going to need more than donuts to get me through the day.*

Born Linwood Robinson, named for his paternal grandfather, Woody had always been the problem child of his straitlaced Baptist family. *You came out the womb trouble, son.* His parents, Doris and John, ran a small church in town. His baby brother, John Jr., had been the golden child. The saving grace in his teens had been Eddie's family, who'd always gone out of their way to welcome him, even when he'd stopped pretending to be anything other than gay.

The rest of the week went on as it always did. Woody had stopped dreaming about winning millions ages ago. Buying the numbers had become more habit than anything else; it also silenced the part of him that always seemed to wonder what if.

And he always bought one for Eddie, who never played the lottery.

Just to aggravate him.

The night of the drawing of the lottery numbers, Woody had fallen asleep in his easy chair in front of the television. *Why bother staying awake?* He'd never gotten more than a hundred bucks from a scratch-off in all his years of gambling.

And honestly, the odds were stacked so far against him. His brother kept telling him to be happy with his lot in life. *Why can't you ever be content with what you have?*

He couldn't.

He'd tried.

There had to be more to life than spending his days building and renovating houses, but maybe banking on a lottery win wasn't the best way of finding it.

A sharp knocking jolted him out of bed long before his alarm clock the following morning. He snagged a wrinkled T-shirt from the floor and dragged it over his head before trudging through the house. *Who the hell is up this early, and where's the fire?*

"Dude. DUDE. *My dude.*"

Woody stared blearily at his best friend and old crush. "I have no idea where your truck is."

Eddie rolled his eyes, clearly not appreciating his attempt at a joke. "Dude. Did you see the news?"

He tried to read the paper being waved violently in front of his face. "If you'd stop flailing, I might get a look at it now."

"You won." Eddie shoved the paper in his face. "You actually did it. Eighty million dollars."

"Are you kidding me?" He stumbled back against the door, the paper falling to the floor at his feet. "Holy shit. I won. If this is a joke, I'm kicking your ass all across the Appalachians."

"You couldn't kick my ass to the mailbox." Eddie grabbed him by the shirt and dragged him into a hug, slapping his back roughly. "It couldn't have happened to a better man."

"I won." Woody repeated the words in his mind over and over; they still didn't quite sink in. "My numbers were right for once. Holy shit. We won. What the hell do we do now? Are we the only winners?"

"Don't lose your ticket." He grinned at him, and Woody's heart skipped a beat as he stepped closer. "Now, I don't want you to think I'm doing this because we've suddenly got money, 'cause I've wanted to do it for years."

"What are—" Woody was cut off by lips crashing against his in an awkward but aggressive first kiss. He caught Eddie by his shirt to keep him from backing away. "Why not give it another shot? Just to celebrate our win?"

The second, third, and fourth kisses went far more smoothly, though no less hungrily. They made out plastered against the front door. Woody hoped none of his neighbors decided to drive by; they might wind up with more of a view than they bargained for.

"I swear I'm not doing this to get a part of your new fortune." Eddie bit playfully at his bottom lip. "It's a nice bonus, though. You can pay for our first date. And yes, we're the only winner. So… how do you feel about splitting eighty million dollars?"

It was Woody's turn to cut him off with another kiss. He stopped counting them, content to know his pure dumb luck hadn't abandoned him after all. *Now, what the hell are we going to do with forty million dollars apiece?*

CHAPTER TWO

EDDIE

"I want no part of whatever you two are fixing to do." Estelle Diaz was Eddie's cousin on his mama's side. She ran the only travel agency in their little town, usually booking trips to places all around the South for local church groups. "Y'all will get me in trouble."

Eddison Howard was the only son born to Edna and Carlton. His older sister, Lanette, had died as a child. He'd grown up with a large, eclectic family led by the indomitable Mama Ester.

Mama Ester had come from Cuba in the sixties and with her daughter, Edna, ran a little diner in a tiny town in South Carolina. She welcomed everyone with open arms and a warm plate of food, and even in her eighties, nothing had changed. Eddie's mom hadn't managed to get her to slow down at all.

"Estelle." Eddie grinned at his cousin. She'd run wild as a child but had grown up into a stunning and strong woman. He tugged on one of her long braids.

"Did you see in the paper about two people winning the lottery in town?"

His cousin immediately turned toward Woody. "Your numbers?"

"Could've been mine."

"You sell tickets. You never buy them. I know Woody always picks up a duplicate ticket for you, though." She speared him with a knowing look. "Did you two finally quit your exhausting little two-step?"

"Mind your business." He winced when she kicked him in the shins. "*Essie.*"

"Don't 'Essie' me, Eddison." She pointed her pencil at him. "Since you've darkened my door, and I highly doubt either of you are interested in touring the grand old churches of Savannah, what do you have in mind?"

Eddie exchanged a glance with Woody, who sat next to him in the comfortable chairs in front of Estelle's little desk. She'd gone for a chic, modern, minimal office. The only pops of color came from artwork highlighting her Cuban-African heritage. "We made lists."

"Lists?" Estelle seemed bewildered as the two men reached into their pockets to retrieve the crumpled sheets of paper. "You couldn't find anything other than a restaurant menu?"

Woody held up his list, which he'd scrawled on the back of a Home Depot receipt. "This better?"

"No, your faded receipt from Home Depot isn't any better." Estelle covered her face with her hand, shaking her head and sending her braids swaying across her shoulders. "You've lost your damn minds."

"Did we have minds to lose?" Woody winked at Eddie, who grinned in return.

"Remember when you told me to shake the Carolina dust off my feet?" Eddie grabbed Woody's list and slid both papers across the desk to his cousin. "Here's our chance."

"Is this receipt from five years ago? Where on earth did you find it?" Estelle peered closely at the paper in her hand.

"In my pocket?"

"I am honestly sorry I asked." She stared at him for several seconds before breaking into laughter. "Bless your heart."

"Can you plan the trip for us?" Eddie was eager to move the conversation on before his new boyfriend and his cousin attempted a sarcasm contest. One Estelle would win.

"It won't be cheap to travel to all these places." She narrowed her deep brown eyes on Eddie. "So, which one of you is the sugar daddy?"

"Essie," Eddie grumbled when she joined Woody in laughing at him. "Going to let Travis and Trey run the store for me. We both won. So, I suppose we're joint daddies? That sounds wrong. Forget I said it."

"Well, if they don't accidentally burn it down in the first week, I'm sure they'll manage just fine without you." Estelle clearly had less confidence in their twenty-two-year-old twin cousins, who'd just graduated from Duke, than he did. She went back to the two lists they'd given her, then lifted a finger to silence them. "This isn't practical, sugar."

"We won the Mega Millions." Woody slouched into the chair. He fished into his pocket and retrieved another thin piece of paper. "See?"

"Practical has a whole new definition." Eddie watched his cousin jot down the country names from their two bucket lists onto a single page in a notebook. "We figured we'd nip the issue of Woody's family suddenly deciding he's not persona non grata by staying on the move. A countrified version of *Around the World in 80 Days*."

Grinning excitedly at the two of them, Estelle moved across her office toward a filing cabinet. She dug through one of the drawers, muttering to herself. Eddie leaned forward to see around her only to narrowly avoid being whacked in the head by the atlas she suddenly held up triumphantly.

"It's not practical in a geographical sense." She opened the book on her desk between them. "You'll waste a lot of time travelling around with the current state of your bucket list."

"And?" He had no doubts she'd already thought of a solution.

"Expand your lists." She pointed to the first country on her notepad. "Uruguay. Why not spend months travelling within an area? Start in Alaska, maybe? It's on both of your lists. Mosey on down through a few places of interest. Take a break, then start all over again in a different part of the world?"

"So, what do we do?" Woody had glanced toward Eddie, who nodded, before asking the question. "I'm not subjecting myself to the aggravation of my folks deciding I'm suddenly a good son because I might give 'em money. They abandoned me; they don't get to want me back because I won the lottery."

"Good. Don't let them mess with you." Estelle patted Woody's hand. She glared pointedly at Eddie. "You take good care of him."

"Me? I'm your cousin." He feigned insult, which sent the three of them laughing. "Do you have any useful suggestions, Essie?"

Estelle grabbed two small notepads from a stack of supplies on a shelf behind her. "Here's what we do. Decide how we're dividing the sections of the world, jot down all the countries or specific cities or attractions you want to visit, and explore within a specific radius around, so there are at least five or six countries per trip. You can come home between each trip to do laundry or whatever else, then head off again."

Closing her travel agency for the day, Estelle called one of their cousins to bring in food from their family restaurant. The three of them crowded around the desk to make plans. They eventually realized some of the countries required visas and specific vaccinations, so those were put down for the third or fourth legs of their journey.

Some of the vaccinations required time or multiple shots. Estelle suggested they make doctor's appointments in the morning. She already had long to-do lists for herself and for them.

Her level of organization amazed and terrified Eddie. He did greatly appreciate her ability to roll with the changes in his life without making a fuss. Not everyone in their little town was likely to be so sweet about it.

"Now what?" Eddie stood slowly out of the chair with a groan, pausing to stretch out his complaining muscles. "We've got our lists."

"I'll begin booking hotels, flights, and transport. You have two jobs. Shop for clothing and gear. Tell your parents that you're going to leave for months at a time." Estelle grinned when he turned his horrified gaze toward her. "I'm sure they'll be fine with their baby boy traipsing around the globe with his boyfriend."

"*Essie.*"

She gave him a double thumbs-up. "Good luck, sugar."

"Don't you dare call any of them." Eddie glared at her, then had to sigh deeply when she simply smiled and waved. "Mothertrucker."

CHAPTER THREE

WOODY

In all his years of moaning about living in a one-stoplight town, Woody had never felt so grateful for his state than when Judge, his old high school buddy turned attorney, had explained that South Carolina allowed lottery winners to accept anonymously. Who wanted their name and photo plastered in every newspaper up and down the East Coast? He'd no doubt a line of previously undiscovered relatives would show up at his door otherwise.

Nope.

Not happening.

He and Eddie had spent the last two days dealing with signing forms in Columbia to get their money and visiting with yet another friend from school who'd become an accountant. Carol Ann had promised to help them deal with taxes and funneling the money into new bank accounts.

I might fumble starting this relationship with Eddie.

I might drop the ball while traveling around the world and embarrass myself.

We're not screwing up our money.

Rough banging on the door jolted him out of his thoughts. A gruff voice shouted from outside, "Open up. I'm hungry. Open the damn door. Linwood?"

Woody rested his head against the top of his kitchen table. He forced himself to his feet, grabbed his coffee, and trudged to the front door. His grinning baby brother stood on the other side. "JJ."

"Little birdy claims someone local won the Mega Millions." JJ pushed by him, heading into the kitchen and opening the fridge. He grabbed a Tupperware of leftovers and started eating cold chicken casserole with his fingers. "Somethin' you wanna share with your brother?"

"Nope." Woody eyed him with a grimace. His brother left a mess in his wake wherever he went. "Don't get your messy fingers all over my kitchen."

"Messy? Me? I heard Ms. Nancy told her daughter who told Momma about you kissing a man by your front door. Not sure what offended her most. The location, the kissing, or the man." JJ continued to shovel leftovers into his mouth with his fingers despite Woody trying to offer a spoon to him. "Daddy's fit to be tied. 'What on earth will the parishioners think of us now?'"

"Are you here to gossip about my love life or the lottery?"

"Both. Called multitasking. Kat goes on and on about being the queen of it."

"Did Kat teach you another SAT word?" Woody

easily blocked the kick JJ aimed at his shins. Katherine, or Kat, had been his brother's high school sweetheart. They'd been together for over fourteen years, married at eighteen right after graduation. "How's she doing?"

"Spitting mad at Momma and Daddy. We look at our girls, you know. They're perfect. And I don't care who they choose to love as long as they're happy. Kat feels the same." JJ paused in his demolishing of the casserole. He always got a proud but terrified look when he talked about his two daughters. "You know we've got your back, right?"

"I know." Woody swallowed down the rush of emotion. His brother would never let him live down shedding a tear. Ever. "Not trying to ruin your relationship with them."

"Don't waste your breath." JJ waved messy fingers at him, making Woody cringe when globs of casserole dripped onto his kitchen floor. "They already ruined everything with their comments about Kitty."

"What now?" Rage already simmered in his belly. Kitty was the oldest of his nieces at seven. She'd recently been diagnosed as autistic, not a surprise given her mother was also on the spectrum. He'd spent several months reading everything available on autism to educate himself. "Is she okay? Should I set them straight?"

"That would end up in a shouting match and someone calling the sheriff." JJ moved over to drop the empty container in the sink and rinsed his fingers off under the tap. "Kat kicked them out of the house after they told Kitty off for flapping her arms when she got excited. They said a few words I won't repeat. Little DeeDee kicked her grandfather in the shins, standing up for her big sister. A shit show. It was a massive pile of manure. They aren't welcome in our home."

Shifting the conversation to his upcoming travels, Woody appreciated his brother not pushing him on the subject of money. He didn't mention he'd set aside trust funds to take care of his nieces' college costs. His lawyer could break the news when Woody was too far away for JJ to yell at him.

His brother, the only family member Woody would gladly give money to, was also the one person who wouldn't ask.

"Why am I not surprised that Estelle told Kat about our trip?" Woody had a feeling their secret had spread through the people she believed were safe to tell. "You're always telling me to settle down or get on with leaving town."

"You are coming home eventually, right?" JJ asked uneasily. He wandered over to the fridge, opening the door and staring inside. "Right?"

"Are you going to miss me?"

JJ glanced over his shoulder at Woody with a mischievous smile. "I've gotta look prettier than someone."

"Did you hit your head again?"

"Kat whacked me with the frying pan." He grabbed a second Tupperware tub, opening it and sniffing at the contents. "Is this safe to eat?"

"Will you stop eating everything in my fridge?"

Woody wondered if he'd have anything left by the time JJ finished.

"Cheapskate. Rolling in dough and you still begrudge your baby brother a meal." JJ sighed dramatically.

"How many meals have you already had and it's not even nine in the morning?"

"I'm a growing boy." JJ took another sniff of the container in his hand. "Does this smell off?"

"Don't you have a business to run? Children to take care of? Groceries to buy? A butt to scratch? Literally anything but annoying me?" Woody regretted opening the door. Though, the last time he didn't answer, his brother had taken the door off the hinges to mess with him. "Construction? Houses to renovate?"

"My only employee just quit." He stared pointedly at his brother before reaching into a drawer for a spoon. "I'll risk it."

"*Dumbass.*"

CHAPTER FOUR

EDDIE

Come over for dinner, sugar.

"Dinner?" Eddie parked outside his parents' home, staring at the familiar vehicles lined up in the driveway. He glanced up at a beep to find Estelle walking away from her shiny purple SUV. "A small family dinner? Sure, Mama. It's a mothertruckin' full-fledged reunion."

"Talking to yourself is never a good sign," Estelle teased. She lifted an errant braid out of her collar. "Don't you glare at me, Eddison."

He narrowed his eyes further on his cousin. "Essie. Who'd you tell?"

"Now, Eddie."

"You two planning on coming inside? Or are you waiting for an invitation?" Their grandmother banged her cane against the porch.

"Yes, Mama Ester," they answered in unison, grinning at each other.

Secrets never stayed hidden for long in a small town.

Eddie wasn't afraid of talking over his plans with his family. They'd always been supportive.

He wanted more time to come up with a game plan. *And an escape route.*

Estelle looped her arm around his, dragging him toward his childhood home. "They're excited you finally made your move on Woody. You know we all love him."

"But?"

His younger cousins, Travis and Trey, dodged by them, singing in harmony about money. Eddie chased after them. Estelle's laughter followed him all the way around the house into the backyard, where his mom and dad were arguing over who grilled the best.

"Slow down before y'all knock over the grill." His mom waved tongs at them. "Leave your cousins alone, Eddison."

"Yes, Mama." He skidded to a halt in front of his parents. He might stand a good foot taller than her, but he had a healthy respect for the fierce woman who'd raised him. He'd inherited her dark brown eyes, and hers glared up at him. "What've I done now?"

She poked him in the chest with the tongs. "I had to wait two whole days to hear from Estelle about you finally getting your man."

"*Mama.*"

"Two. Whole. Days."

"I thought we didn't lie in our house?" Eddie grinned at her. "Am I really supposed to believe Estelle managed to keep this big of a secret for more than an hour?"

She poked him again with the tongs. "Help your cousins set the table."

He gave her a hug before running off with one of the finished beef patties. She made the best burgers, a fusion of Cuban-American flavors that danced across the tongue. "Yes, Mama."

"Don't talk with your mouth full."

Winking at his cousins, Eddie made quick work of the burger. He brushed his hands clean on Trey's shirt, much to his indignation. They wrestled playfully until a shrill whistle from his dad settled them down.

The dreaded family discussion never happened. Eddie had expected to be cornered sometime during the meal. Instead, they all sat outside enjoying the slightly cooler weather September had brought to the end of a sweltering hot summer.

Eddie had never been overly ambitious like some of his cousins. All he wanted was family, friends, love, and stability. The gas station had provided a good life for him. He had a wealth of riches, in his mind.

A large family who loved one another deeply.

A strong-knit group of friends.

His business was moderately successful.

But falling in love?

Love had been the one point of failure in his life. Eddie had dated a number of men over the years, unfulfilling relationships that ended before they'd begun for one simple reason. None of them had been Woody.

And in the end, he'd realized it had always been Woody.

Not an earth-shattering epiphany. They'd always

had a connection. Best friends from practically day one. Hell, every time Woody bought a lottery ticket, he purchased one for Eddie because he'd always claimed not to want to go anywhere without him.

And now we're going to travel the world.

Good lord, here's hoping we don't get arrested for having sex somewhere we shouldn't.

As dinner ended, the sun had gone down, leaving crickets chirping in the twilight. He helped his dad get a fire going in the pit in the corner of the yard. They sat around, making jokes and enjoying the *pastelitos de guayaba* his grandmother had baked for them, a Cuban pastry Mama Ester made on special occasions.

"Eddison."

He sat up in the wooden deck chair, focusing his attention on his dad across the roaring fire. "Sir?"

"We all agree you and Woody should go on your year of adventure. Secrets don't stay quiet in this town. Everyone's going to know y'all have money. They'll hound you for ages. Go. Explore." His dad had clearly been deemed the spokesman for the family. "Don't get arrested or in trouble. And keep your money to yourself. We're fine."

"I…." Eddie trailed off when his dad raised a hand to silence him. "All right."

I'll just do what Woody did: make plans with Carol Ann to set aside funds for all of them.

I won't be here to hear them complaining.

And they'll complain. They've got master's degrees in the art of guilt trips.

CHAPTER FIVE

WOODY

"Who's going to mow your lawn?" Eddie tapped his bottle against Woody's leg, waking him out of his doze. "Lawn? Mowing? Earth to Linwood?"

"I heard you," Woody grumbled. Eddie had brought leftovers from his dinner with the family the day before, along with beer, to fuel their evening of trip planning. They hadn't quite yet gotten beyond food, beer, and making out like horny teenagers in Woody's backyard. "Kat's going to have one of her cousins come over every couple of weeks. I gotta remember to leave a chunk of change with her to pay the kid."

"So, Alaska."

"Smooth transition." Woody easily blocked the lazy punch Eddie threw at his arm. He shifted his chair closer to Eddie before tossing a log onto his fire pit. The chairs had been borrowed from his brother ten years ago; JJ hadn't missed them yet. "Alaska. We're making a point not to get our tongues or any other parts frozen to any inanimate objects. Anything else?"

"I'd risk hypothermia to fuck under the northern lights."

Woody inhaled his beer and coughed violently. He shoved Eddie out of his chair. "We might traumatize the polar bears."

"Well, you're almost a bear. Not quite."

"Ha, ha, ha. Workout goals." Woody finally managed to get his coughing under control. "We should make a bucket list of all the places we want to have sex on our journey. Number one? My backyard, under the stars, in front of this fire. Northern lights can be a close second."

"Patience never was much of a virtue for either of us."

"Hey! Linwood. We're coming back. And by we, I mean me and the miniatures. Y'all better have clothes on your bodies." JJ's voice boomed from toward the front of the house. "Woody?"

"We heard you. My neighbors heard you." Woody had a feeling the entire town would hear eventually, given the gossipy nature of the folks who lived a few yards over. "We're decent."

"Clothed, at least." Eddie reached into the cooler beside him to pull out a few more beers. He handed one over to Woody. "Isn't there a time limit on when family can bother you?"

"Your mom brought you breakfast. Us. Breakfast. At your house. And you want to talk about boundaries?" Woody hadn't known whether to be embarrassed or grateful. "Ain't no time limit on when family comes over.

Not here, anyway. It'll be harder when we're halfway around the world."

"Thank God for that." Eddie waved at JJ, who had a daughter on his shoulders and another one clinging to his leg giggling. "Beer?"

"Uncle Woody. Uncle Eddie." Kitty waved enthusiastically from her father's shoulders. Her little sister grinned at them while encouraging JJ to walk faster. "We had ice cream. Shh. Don't tell Mom."

Woody grabbed DeeDee from his brother's leg and tossed her up into the air, then hugged her tightly. "You do realize these two will rat you out the second you get home, right? Adorable, but loose-lipped."

The two girls ran around in the twilight. They clambered over the jungle gym Woody had set up in his yard just for them. JJ grabbed one of the spare lawn chairs and waved off the beer Eddie offered.

JJ had a hard rule of never drinking and driving, particularly with the girls in the car. "Kat sent me over."

"What'd you do this time?" Woody kept an eye on his nieces while teasing his baby brother.

Turned out JJ hadn't done anything. Kat had overheard a pair of ladies gossiping at the grocery store. She'd sent him out as soon as he finished his last job to warn Woody.

"Momma and Daddy know you won the lottery. You know they'll be wanting part of it." JJ waved his girls away from the swings. "I'm gonna get these two home. Just, maybe spend a few days in Columbia preparing for your trip."

Eddie waited until goodbyes and hugs had been

exchanged before turning to Woody. "We need a list. Preferably one not written on a Home Depot receipt that's older than Methuselah."

"Were there a lot of DIY shops in those days?" Woody doused the fire with a bucket of rainwater he kept handy. "I've got a notebook in the house somewhere. We can make a list, then drive out to Columbia for a shopping spree. Are your cousins up for handling the gas station for you already?"

"They've worked for me every summer since they were old enough. They'll manage." Eddie caught him by his belt loop, dragging him into the house. "Are we really going to do this? Travel the world? Spend more money than either of us could've dreamed of on a vacation?"

"We are." He met Eddie's brown eyes confidently. "Don't call it a vacation. We've worked our asses off our whole lives. This is our chance to run away without guilt —see everything the world has to offer together. We've buried ourselves in this little town, ignoring the painful truth."

"What painful truth?"

"We were so damn scared to admit we loved each other that we wasted almost twenty years of our lives pretending to be *just* friends." Woody blinked a few times before clearing his throat. He pushed by Eddie to move through the cramped hallway into the kitchen. "Gotta be a notepad around here somewhere."

"Woody?"

Ignoring the call, Woody pulled out one drawer after the other. He closed the last one, only to find himself forcefully turned around and pushed against the cabinets. Eddie had gripped him firmly by the arms to hold him there.

"No, no. You don't drop love into a conversation, then start digging around in your kitchen drawers like nothing happened." Eddie licked his bottom lip, and Woody found his gaze glued to the sight. "How does traveling the world together help us?"

Woody shrugged. He leaned forward, lips curving up into a grin. "You aren't disagreeing with me."

"My mama taught me to always tell the truth." Eddie glanced over his shoulder. "Found a notebook."

They eased away from each other. Woody snagged the blue notebook and a pen. Eddie grabbed a bag of chips and a pack of Oreos.

"Sustenance." He also grabbed the carton of milk from the fridge. "What are we doing?"

"Making a list of whatever we need in Alaska." Woody sat on the floor by his coffee table. He turned on the TV to watch a replay of a recent football game. "Do you have the email from Estelle on the first leg of our trip?"

Eddie dropped down to sit beside him. Their legs pressed together. "Alaska, Montana, and somewhere in Canada. We'll come back home for laundry, then head down to South America."

Woody jotted down the specific cities, parks, and areas for his own reference. "Right. We'll need hiking gear. Layers. Lots of layers."

"Layers?"

"Kat always talks about layers." Woody shrugged.

"You've no idea what you're talking about, do you?" Eddie snickered.

"Do you have a better idea?"

"Of course." Eddie tilted his phone for Woody to see. "Found a website that lists everything needed to visit Alaska."

"Cheater."

They polished off the chips, cookies, and a full gallon of milk between them. Their messy writing filled four pages of the notebook. Most of the items had been copied directly from a backpacker website.

"Would you ever have told me?"

Woody moved his full attention from the list over to Eddie, who was lounging beside him on the carpet. "Would you have told me?"

Eddie twirled the pen around his fingers, reminding Woody of the summer they'd spent teaching themselves tricks to annoy their ninth-grade math teacher. "I don't know."

"Well, thank the stars for my pure dumb luck. Or we'd be horny, alone, and pathetic."

CHAPTER SIX

EDDIE

OVER THE COURSE OF THEIR HIGH SCHOOL FOOTBALL career, they'd traveled frequently. As adults, they'd gone on fishing trips together. Eddie had never experienced a moment of anxiety over any of those trips, not about Woody's presence.

He'd cleaned his truck, inside and out. His barber cousin had trimmed up his beard and hair. Estelle had invaded his home (and closet) to find the perfect outfit for him, laughing the entire time.

The jeans did fit nicely. The shirt *did* drape over his shoulders to perfectly highlight his muscles. Estelle seemed far too pleased with herself, so he pushed her snickering self out the front door.

Collapsing back on the couch with a groan, Eddie tried to process the bizarre turn his life had taken. He was a millionaire. And so was his best friend.

Millionaires.

Winning had been a shock. Woody's insistence on

his coming along for the wild ride hadn't. For better or worse, they'd always done everything together.

We should count our blessings that this happened in our late thirties. We would've flown through every single penny if millions had been dropped in our laps in our teens when Woody started buying tickets for both of us.

Carol Ann had promised to help with his finances as well. She'd coordinate with Judge to provide both Eddie and Woody with the best bang for their buck. They'd both combined funds of a significant amount into a joint account just for their epic adventure. The remainder was put into savings accounts to deal with when they came home.

If we return home.

The one exception had been trust accounts. Taking a note from Woody, Eddie had set up several for his family. Carol Ann could tell them after he left.

Yes, yes, we are cowards.

Rich cowards.

Eddie had always been the more realistic and less optimistic of the two of them. Woody, despite his parent's reaction, saw the good. Eddie knew not all their friends, family, and neighbors would be thrilled over their change in relationship status.

Maybe I should switch my Facebook status just to screw with them.

He knew some would think the trip was them running away from their problems.

Can I live my life worrying about handling a bunch of horseshit?

Nope.

I sure as hell can't.

Sleep never came easily to Eddie. He exhausted himself with going through his closet and thinking about all the little tasks, like making sure bills were on auto pay. *Or shit, we can just pay everything off. That's going to take some getting used to.* He wondered if Woody had even considered it.

He eventually drifted off on the floor, surrounded by piles of clothing. His attempt at organization hadn't worked out as planned. He had managed to decide what *not* to bring to Alaska.

Waking up with a crick in his neck, Eddie rolled over on his back. He stared up at a cobweb on the ceiling for several minutes. The familiar sound of truck tires on his gravel driveway forced him to make an effort to sit up.

"It's open," he yelled out a minute later when footsteps drew close to the door.

"You are so country," Woody drawled, stepping over the piles of clothing to sit on a clear spot on the couch. "I lock my doors at night."

"Only because your parents used to show up randomly while you were working and throw out anything they thought a God-fearing man shouldn't own." Eddie grinned at him. "Remember the time we bought all those porn VHS tapes and magazines to leave around for them to find?"

Woody threw his head back, laughing deeply and loudly. "Pretty sure they heard Momma's scream three counties over."

It was Eddie's favorite laugh in the world and never failed to make his dick hard. His voice was smooth as silk, but Woody's went low and deep, a sexy balm to his soul even at the worst of times.

"Any reason why you've dumped your closet onto the living room floor?" Woody reached down to snag a football jersey. "How the hell do you still have your high school jersey?"

"You can kiss my grass. Stop judging me." Eddie snatched it away from him. "Midnight seemed like the perfect time to determine what I want to bring on this insane trip."

"Trouble sleeping?" Woody's gaze turned sympathetic. Eddie focused on badly refolding the jersey before giving up and tossing it onto one of the piles. "What happened to the sleep study the doc wanted you to do?"

"Insurance wouldn't cover it. Mama Ester wanted to pay for me." Eddie had lied to his grandma, told her he'd changed his insurance's mind. He hadn't, but taking her money felt wrong. "Guess I don't have to worry about the cost now."

"No, you don't." Woody gave him a look that told him if they didn't head out the door, they'd be leaving for Columbia several hours later than intended.

Eddie placed a hand on Woody's shoulder to turn him toward the door. He patted himself on the back for packing for their impromptu trip in the middle of the night. "Don't even start. Keep your tongue in your mouth and your dick in your pants."

"You're a stealer of fun. Fun stealer," Woody grumbled.

Eddie grabbed his bag and led the way out of the

house. He froze outside of the door, causing Woody to bump into him. "Mothertrucker."

"What now?" Woody shoved him out of the way, only to halt midstep as well. "Damn it all."

"Watch your language, son."

"Why? I'm too old for you to wash my mouth out with soap." Woody walked over to grab his bag from the back of his truck, strode over to Eddie's Silverado, and peered into the gleaming paint. "Damn it all."

Eddie chuckled, ignoring the outraged glares from the esteemed—in their own minds—Reverend Robinson and his Tammy Faye-wannabe missus. "You're blocking my drive."

"Your daddy and I wanted to talk with you." Doris Robinson didn't even acknowledge Eddie's presence. She grabbed her son by the arm. "It's been such a long time. We're ready to welcome you back home. God's calling you, Linwood."

Woody was polite to a fault with his family. "Is he?" Mostly the cliché of a southern gentleman with a side of cowboy rocker thrown in for good measure.

Eddie didn't have any of the internal conflicted emotions requiring him to be polite—and definitely not to someone who'd gone out of their way to hurt Woody.

My Woody.

Or, maybe my Linwood.

Sounds less thirstily creepy.

My Woody.

Don't laugh.

"Son? Your momma's talking to you."

Eddie rolled his shoulders and stepped forward into

the poor excuse for a preacher's face. Woody's parents were a bruise that had been pressed continuously, making his usually long fuse short. He'd always felt the need to step between Woody and the holier-than-thou duo. "I don't appreciate the tone in your voice. And I don't *appreciate* your presence. Get off my property."

John had to tilt his head to meet Eddie's eyes and stumbled backwards, reaching for his wife to pull her away. "You—"

"Shut your pie hole." Eddie pointed toward the Buick blocking his driveway. He suddenly didn't see any reason to put up with them. They'd tossed their son into the trash; why should they care now? "Take Tammy Faye and go find someone who can be bothered to give a damn."

"Linwood?" Woody's mother broke the stunned silence.

Ignoring his parents, Woody got into the passenger side of the Silverado. Eddie watched in silence until the Robinsons left. He hopped into his truck, put the key into the ignition, and turned toward Woody, only for his concern to be dashed away with the most aggressively intense kiss he'd ever experienced.

He breathlessly licked his bottom lip when Woody released him. "Right. So, Columbia?"

"Might as well grab coffee and a breakfast sandwich from your family's restaurant." Woody pulled at his T-shirt a little, obviously trying to straighten his appearance. "Columbia?"

"And then… the world."

"I worry about you." Woody grinned at him.

CHAPTER SEVEN

WOODY

Since neither of them enjoyed shopping, even with increased funds, they approached their to-do list in Columbia with the precision of drill instructors. At their first shop, they'd met a young lesbian who ran the place, Sharon, who'd spent a year backpacking across the world. Her advice adjusted their plans and their list of items to buy.

After learning cost wasn't an issue, Sharon had immediately crossed out their chosen bags, suggesting a more expensive but waterproof and lockable pack from Tortuga. She'd insisted on packing cubes, telling them they'd thank her later. Her journey had included time in the frozen tundra, so they listened carefully to all her ideas.

Woody realized quickly they'd gone into the idea of traveling and hiking for a year without a sufficient amount of knowledge. He had a whispered conversation with Eddie then asked if Sharon might play the role of shopping guide, for a fee. They had the money, needed the help, and weren't too proud to ask for it.

At the end of their three days in the city, Woody stared in awe at the bags strewn across their hotel bed. Sharon had been an angel. She'd even taken them out in the evening twice to introduce them to the gay-friendly scene in Columbia. They'd enjoyed The Art Bar, and Woody had had the pleasure of watching Eddie sing karaoke.

A rare treat, since Eddie usually refused to sing for anyone.

Sleeping together in bed had been yet another treat. Woody had watched Eddie drift off, unbothered by insomnia for once. He found himself choked by emotion at the idea they might never have had the courage to love.

He'd initially thought they'd spend all their time screwing after what felt like a lifetime of abstinence. *Dial back the drama, Woody; we weren't wearing chastity rings.* It was different, though. And somehow, he'd always known it would be with Eddie.

Always.

Estelle and JJ had both kept up a steady stream of text messages to them. Woody's parents hadn't handled receiving a dose of their own medicine well. In his brother's words, they'd thrown a full-on toddler tantrum, expecting both JJ and many in their little town to side with them.

He'd been genuinely touched (and surprised) when JJ shared a short video of one of the church deacons reading the reverend the riot act for throwing his own child away. *Judge not lest ye be judged.* His holier-than-thou parents had been skewered by their own weapon —religion.

A week later, they sat once again in Estelle's travel agency. JJ, Kat, Mama Ester, and Eddie's parents had joined them. Estelle had closed her office for the day to go over their timetable for the last time and celebrate their going away.

Mama Ester had pulled Woody aside, patting his cheeks with her slightly trembling fingers. "You take care of my Eddison, you hear me?"

"Yes, ma'am." Woody kissed her cheek and pulled her into a gentle hug. "You take care of yourself. We'll come by to visit as often as possible. I promise."

"Good. And you take care of yourself as well. Never mind all that horse manure your momma and daddy have spread around town. Everyone who loves you knows they haven't got the good sense God gave a goose." Mama Ester slipped a ten-dollar bill into his head. "Now, you take my grandson out for a nice meal before your flight."

Woody knew better than to argue with her. She'd been slipping him money since his parents disowned him, despite him now being a grown adult in his late thirties. "Yes, ma'am. Do geese have any good sense?"

Mama Ester waggled her finger at him. "You behave yourself."

"Yes, ma'am." He grinned when she whacked him on the arm with her massive purse.

They planned to spend a few weeks in Alaska, then a few in Montana hiking trails in Glacier National Park before heading north to Canada. Eddie, in particular, had wanted to see the Plain of Six Glaciers—if the weather held. Going in October might be pushing their luck.

Estelle promised to keep an eye on the weather and monitor the park website. If Banff National Park closed early, they'd push their trip to Peru up. September in Alaska, October in Montana and Canada. Their goal was to hit Peru and Easter Island by November.

"Are you excited about flying?" Kat slid up beside him with one of her daughters in her arms, already asleep despite the noise in the room.

Woody flapped his arms at his side. "Might get tired."

Kat rolled her eyes and stared up at the ceiling. "Bless your heart."

He wrapped an arm around his quietly laughing sister-in-law. "Keep an eye on JJ, will you?"

"Always do," she said fiercely.

And she would. Kat had always been a strong mama bear. She also had more sense than his baby brother, who tended to allow their parents to walk all over him.

They ate their weight in BBQ brought by Eddie's family. Woody couldn't resist the siren call of the marinated shredded mojo pork. He did wonder at the wisdom of stuffing themselves with a long day of travel ahead of them the following morning.

Hugs.

Tears.

More hugs.

Woody finally wound up sitting alone in his truck

after everyone had left, staring at the dark travel agency in front of him. Eddie had driven home with his dad to park his Silverado at his family home. "Well, we're doing it."

Pulling onto the street, Woody went on a slow drive around their sleepy town. He'd miss aspects of living in his small, refurbished farmhouse. Kat's words of encouragement came back to him as he made his way home.

You deserve happiness. And love. You're worthy. Maybe it was pure dumb luck, but you still deserve every door now open to you.

I know you've got enough sense to not cut your nose off to spite your face.

He did have plenty of sense.

He'd channeled all those feelings of unworthiness into a mediocre life, afraid to rock the boat fully. Now he had the chance to blast it out of the water.

And the only thing causing him to hesitate was parents who'd stopped caring the moment he came out.

Had they ever loved him?

Fuck 'em.

I don't owe them another moment of my happiness.

I'm going to travel the world—and screw Eddie in every country we can.

Morning came far too quickly. Woody had barely fallen asleep before the alarm went off at four. JJ showed up twenty minutes later; Kat had clearly woken him up on time.

"Isn't there a clause in the brother handbook that says I can't be required to wake up before seven in the morning?" JJ rested his forehead against the steering wheel as they waited for Eddie. He'd grumbled the entire drive from Woody's place over to the Howard home. "There are bacon, egg, and cheese biscuits in the paper bag. Kat worried you might not remember to eat breakfast."

"You didn't have to give us a ride," Woody pointed out. He fished one of the sandwiches out of the bag, handing it over to his brother. Kat had made six. She knew their appetites well. "And you volunteered."

"I clearly took leave of my senses." JJ practically inhaled his breakfast. "Where's your tall drink of water? Go wake him up."

"Do you want to risk annoying Carlton Howard?" Woody still remembered the time as teenagers when they'd borrowed and then wrecked the Howard family car. They'd gone over a hill too fast, lost control, went into the air, and straight into a ditch. Mr. Howard had *not* been happy with them. "I don't."

"Coward."

Woody rolled his eyes at his brother. "Right. I'm the coward? Who leaves his dirty work boots outside the front door to avoid angering his wife?"

"It's called respect." JJ punched his brother in the leg. "You're a— Oh hey, Mama Ester made breakfast."

And she had. Eddie had appeared with a paper plate of tostadas and a large thermos of what Woody knew would be *café con leche*. Grilled Cuban bread and even more coffee. They'd definitely be awake by the time they arrived in Columbia to grab the first of two flights.

JJ watched with him as the Howards bid their son goodbye with tears and hugs. He glanced over at Woody.

"Do you ever wish Momma and Daddy were like them?"

"All the goddamn time," Woody admitted with a slight ache in his heart. "All the *goddamn* time."

Eddie

"Well, too late to back out now." Eddie stood shoulder to shoulder with Woody, staring at the crowded seating area outside of their gate at the Atlanta airport. Their drive to Columbia and the short flight to GA had gone well. Now, though, the reality of cold, ice, and adventure had hit him. "Are we really going to Alaska?"

Woody grabbed him by the arm to drag him forward as the airline gate person called out for first class passengers. "We can't wimp out now. Not after JJ driving us all the way to Columbia at four in the morning. You know how irate my brother would be?"

With a chuckle, Eddie followed him. They offered their tickets and made their way toward the airplane. He found a strange enjoyment in the nervous energy building up in him; they really were going to travel the world in style.

Together.

Mothertrucker.

Lord have mercy.

Here's hoping we don't get our stupid asses arrested.

They were seated in the last row of first class, offering what felt like a bit of privacy. The extra leg room kept Eddie from having to squash his six-foot-plus frame in like a sardine.

By the time they'd settled into the seven-hour flight, Eddie had wrapped his mind around being in first-class seats and their impending adventure. It was becoming real. Not some bizarre dream. He shifted slightly in the seat, reaching forward to take a sip of the beer the flight attendant had poured for him.

Aren't we fancy?

A far cry from drinking from a mason jar and seeing how far we can spit sunflower seeds across the back lot.

Leaning back in the seat with a blanket across his lap, Eddie started to drift off to sleep. He jolted fully awake when a hand dropped on his leg. His gaze immediately went to Woody, who lifted an eyebrow in obvious question, wanting consent to move forward.

With most of the windows closed and their overhead lights off, Eddie hoped no one noticed the arm stretched out underneath the blankets. They'd have a hard time explaining the hand that had begun to lower the zipper of his jeans.

Woody's fingers slowly slipped around Eddie's dick, which definitely stood up to pay attention. They froze anytime someone walked by. Eddie had to clench his teeth to keep from uttering a sound.

Crud muffin.

Smirking son of a bitch.

Smirking while casually reclining in his seat, Woody didn't appear at all flustered by jacking Eddie off in their first-class seats. Eddie, on the other hand, hadn't felt so flustered since getting caught making out by his parents. Joining the mile-high club had not been on his bucket list.

Apparently, it was now.

Those fingers were maddening. They danced around the head of his cock. He had no idea how Woody managed to move subtly enough not to be noticed, yet more than enough to bubble up the pleasure deep in his belly.

"Wood."

"Yep, that's what I'm playing with." Woody continued to smirk at him. Eddie promised himself he'd get revenge at some point. "Maybe we won't write home about this part."

"You—" Eddie clenched his mouth shut, keeping in the moan that wanted out. Woody had twisted his fingers around, and the jolt of wicked pleasure knocked the air out of him. "Damn it."

"Shh. Don't draw their attention. They'll think we want another beer," Woody teased. "Wouldn't want me to leave you high and dry?"

"You're going to leave me tired and wet," Eddie muttered. He had to forcibly keep his hips from shifting up into the fingers now gliding slowly down his shaft. "*Linwood.*"

The sensations those calloused fingers sent through him were as strong as any Eddie had ever experienced. He let himself sink into the feeling. The lazy stroking kept him just hovering on the edge of satisfaction.

"Steady, Ed." Woody kept his grip on Eddie. "Don't give the game away too early. Keep your eye on the ball."

"Not eyes I want on my balls." He wished they had more privacy, enough for him to get a hold of Woody to share.

No way two six-foot-plus men were sneaking into the bathroom. They'd barely fit on their own, let alone both of them. Someone would definitely notice.

Might be funny as hell.

Might be worth getting tossed out on our ear.

Maybe not. Let's not start our journey with a trip in the back of a police car for fucking in an airplane toilet.

Woody drew out the moment until Eddie thought the teasing would drive him to the brink of insanity. "Ready to check the first item on my bucket list?"

"What?" Eddie was barely holding on to his ability to breathe normally.

"Orgasm at thirty-five-thousand feet."

And Eddie did.

In his briefs, ones that he'd definitely be removing so he could go commando for the rest of the flight.

His trip to the bathroom felt like the walk of shame he'd done in college once. He managed to sneakily get his boxers off and shoved into his pocket, and cleaned himself up without much fuss. With some luck, he managed to sneak the underwear into his carry-on—and not drop them into the aisle, despite Woody reaching out to tickle him on the side.

That's two things to get payback for.

Revenge will be sweet.

"Stop plotting. You're more Mini-Me than Dr. Evil."

Four hours later, they'd arrived at the Anchorage airport. They carried their backpacks outside to grab their rental. Eddie stared out into the Alaskan sky, glad he'd kept a jacket easily accessible.

"Well?"

Eddie glanced over at Woody, who had a grin on his face. "Let's do it."

"Ride off into the sunset?"

Eddie shoved Woody. "Take our first steps into this grand adventure."

"One small—" Woody took off at a run with a shouting Eddie following.

CHAPTER EIGHT

WOODY

After picking up their rental, they drove to their hotel for the next few days. The Captain Cook. Estelle had made all of their reservations. Neither of them had actually seen any of the hotels booked.

Or had a clue about the rooms.

Stepping out of the elevator onto the private floor into a one-bedroom suite in the Crow's Nest at the top of the third tower of the luxury hotel was a kick in the pants. Woody dumped his backpack on the most expensive-looking couch he'd ever seen and stumbled over to one of the large windows to stare across downtown Anchorage.

Eddie stepped up beside him, throwing an arm across his shoulders. "Welcome to the millionaires' club."

"I'm afraid to fucking touch anything." Woody stared at the mountains in the distance with a sense of awe. "I've been running full blast since you showed me the winning numbers—and now I think reality is finally hitting me. I'm a millionaire. We are."

"Not sure reality is the word." Eddie dropped his arm away and leaned forward to rest his head against the glass. "Did you see the suits hanging in the closet?"

"Suits?"

Woody wandered toward the nicest hotel bedroom he'd ever seen. He stepped around the backpacks Eddie had obviously set on the floor. "There's a note."

"You could read it instead of staring at it like you stare at my ass."

"Your ass isn't as flat as a piece of paper." Woody deftly dodged Eddie when he went for a tackle, sending the six-foot-two former football player crashing into the bed. "You break it, you bought it."

"Just read the note."

"Dear Fools, the concierge helped me organize suits for you since your dinner reservations require business casual at a minimum. Not the wrinkled jeans and T-shirts you're wearing. Don't embarrass yourselves. Love, Essie." Woody waved the printed-out paper that appeared to be from an email Estelle had sent to the hotel. "Did you know hotels would pick up clothes for you?"

"Money talks."

Woody checked out both suits, finding one had "Mr. Robinson" attached to the coat hanger. He grabbed both and handed Eddie's to him. "I'm Richard Gere."

"I think we're both Julia Roberts, and Essie is Richard Gere."

"Essie's the hotel concierge. What was his name? Hector Elizondo?"

"Pretty sure we're more *Beverly Hillbillies* than *Pretty Woman*." Eddie held the suit in front of him. "Is this us?"

"Essie made the reservations." Woody knew Eddie's cousin wanted them to experience everything the world had to offer. Eddie stared at him over the top of the suit. "And we might be eating beef jerky and cold beans while we're hiking."

"Yeah, but it's teriyaki-flavored jerky." He'd made sure to pack at least four bags in their supplies.

Woody stared down at the suit. He traced his fingers along the collar. Part of him wanted to blow off the idea of a fancier meal and enjoy a greasy burger and fries, but another, hornier side of him wanted to see Eddie all dressed up. "Essie'll never let us hear the end of it if we blow off all her hard work."

Eddie sighed deeply before carefully draping the suit across the bed. "This better not be one of those places that serve tiny food. I'm starving."

They barely had enough time to get showered and dressed if there weren't any distractions. Unfortunately, Woody found a naked Eddie incredibly distracting. They made it to the restaurant twenty minutes late.

Thankfully, Woody found slipping a fifty brightened the mood of the maître d' significantly.

Everyone's happy.

Seated at a table looking over the inlet, Woody tried to nod in all the right places when the sommelier rambled on about their selection of wines. Eddie was definitely trying not to laugh. He avoided meeting his gaze to keep from breaking.

The menu was intimidating.

What the hell is foie gras?

Just remember, you can always have pizza delivered.

They went with the charcuterie for a starter. Eddie wanted to try duck bacon. Woody eyed the pâté suspiciously, but they found everything tasted amazing.

As they made their way through appetizers and salads, Woody found himself impatient for the main course. King crab. Bison filet. Beef rib eye. They'd gotten the rib eye to share. He could only stare in amazement at the size of the dishes, regretting for an instant how much of the starter he'd consumed.

The king crab legs were almost a religious experience. Woody decided to throw himself fully into every experience on this journey—no matter how large or small. Dinner overlooking the harbor in downtown Anchorage definitely qualified.

"Trade you a leg for part of your bison." Woody offered one of them to Eddie, hoping for more than just a taste of the filet. He held up the crab to cover his mouth. "Crab smile?"

Eddie snapped a photo with his phone. "Not sure the stuffed shirts approve of our clowning around."

"We'll tip well."

"Does this make us nouveau riche?" Eddie grinned. He cut a piece off his filet and slipped it onto Woody's plate. "Sending the photo to Essie. She'll appreciate seeing the fruits of her labor."

"Or she'll text you a lengthy lecture on table

manners." Woody had ignored that page in the book Estelle had put together for the Alaska, Montana, and Canada section of their journey. "Think we could save one of these legs to ship to her?"

"Tempting." Eddie snapped a photo of his own meal.

Dessert turned out to be a second trip to nirvana. Chocolate cake. Woody had eaten a million different versions. He'd never had one that tasted like velvet, dark chocolate sex. He almost stabbed Eddie with his fork when he tried to steal a bite.

"Sharing is caring," Eddie grumbled.

"We're not in kindergarten. And this sure as shit isn't crayons or Lego." Woody wrapped his arms around the plate. "I am a dragon. And my hoard is cake."

"Your hoard is going to get moldy." Eddie sparred with him, dueling with forks until Woody finally let him have a bite. "Mothertrucker."

With extreme self-control, Woody talked himself out of seconds on the cake. They'd be wandering around Anchorage tomorrow and the day after heading south to Seward to hike a glacier. He didn't think extra chocolate would help.

They trudged back to their room, sliding to the plush carpet on the floor. Woody undid his belt and groaned. Eddie flopped over so they lay side by side.

"Ed?"

"Hmm?"

"Will all of this ever feel normal to us?" Woody had enjoyed dinner but also felt like a country bumpkin trying to decide which fork to use first.

"Who cares?" Eddie shifted slightly and turned his head toward him. "I don't. Do you?"

"No, but—"

"Shut your pie hole and listen to me," Eddie insisted. "Did you suddenly change your personality and character because you won the lottery?"

"Well, no."

"Then stop making mountains out of ant hills. Besides, you were never completely normal anyway. This won't change a thing."

"Dickhead." Woody had made all these plans to seduce Eddie after dinner. He'd been unable to resist fantasizing while watching Eddie in his suit. Now, he didn't even want to move, let alone attempt to see if his cock was interested. "Just leave me to die here in food bliss."

"Here lie two millionaires. They never made it past their first meal." Eddie snickered. "They really liked the crab legs."

CHAPTER NINE

EDDIE

Six in the morning. Day four of our Alaska journey. Suits gone. Hiking boots laced up. Let's get our glacier on.

Worst pep talk in history?

Probably.

Yesterday they'd driven the three hours from Anchorage to a lodge in Seward. It would be their base camp for the next ten days. They'd already walked the easy lower trail in the Kenai Fjords National Park. It gave them a peek at the glacier and allowed them to stretch their legs in preparation for harder paths.

Today would not be a cake walk. The Harding Icefield Trail offered a challenging hike of over eight miles. They planned to make a day of enjoying the stunningly beautiful weather and views.

"Excited?" Woody wandered naked into the bathroom, sliding into the shower behind him. "See you snuck in here to use up all the hot water."

They'd discovered the hard way their cabin only had so much hot water. Eddie had frozen his balls off after

Woody hogged the shower. He promised not to make the same mistake again.

"Getting there." Eddie inhaled sharply when Woody wrapped his fingers around Eddie's shaft. "Well, morning to you too."

Having denied themselves for so long, Eddie found they had their hands on each other more often than not. He'd feared it would be awkward. Or worse, having wanted a relationship for so long, reality might be disappointing.

It wasn't.

Sleeping together felt natural. Eddie had been stunned at waking up the first time beside Woody, having slept through the night. It seemed his cure for insomnia had been a good meal, sex, and a Woody-sized teddy bear.

Their long history as friends had transitioned beautifully into more. More than Eddie had imagined possible. Though, fucking Woody against the tile wall had featured in his imagination frequently.

After finishing up in the shower, they grabbed a quick breakfast, double-checked their hiking gear, and made the short drive to the parking area at the nature center. They'd hoped to get on the trail early, given the roundtrip journey would likely take a good eight hours. Neither of them wanted to rush their way through the woods and glacier.

Life is all about the living, right?

If we're racing by, who knows what views we might miss in the rush to get to the end and say we did it.

"Ready?" Woody secured his backpack and grabbed

his walking stick. They'd picked up the sturdy, collapsible trekking poles at a store in Anchorage. "Got your stick?"

"I'll stick you." Eddie whacked Woody on the behind with his. He had a feeling, given the number of hikes planned for their future, the walking poles would get plenty of use. "Let's get going, if we're lucky, we'll get ahead of the first ranger-led group."

They moved relatively quickly from the initial flat path into the narrow trail leading through the forest. As the incline steepened, Eddie caught glimpses of the stunning views across the valley. They stopped periodically to get their cameras out.

He'd doubted Estelle's insistence on them buying a decent point-and-shoot camera. Now, with the first view of the glacier, he had to admit his cousin had been right. They'd have kicked themselves if they didn't have photographs to bring home with them.

Memories.

"Water?"

Eddie was jolted from his thoughts as they picked their way carefully over the loose rocks on the switch-backs, guiding them higher and higher to the Harding Icefield. He took a swig of water before dragging Woody over for a kiss. More than, since tongues were involved. A show for the other hikers moving by them, if the cheers and whistles were anything to go by. "There. We've made out at altitude."

After a strenuous climb, they found a spot amidst the rocks to sit and take in the spectacular view. He glanced across the valley below, flashes of white from the snow and the glacier itself contrasting against the blue sky above. It took his breath away, the awe-inspiring beauty of it all.

How many times in the next year will I look out across a vista and be stunned by how damned lucky we are?

"Ed?" Woody nudged him in the arm before waving a protein bar in front of his face. "You all right there?"

"Just…." He trailed off, unsure of how to explain, and gestured once again to the ice fields. They'd overheard one of the park rangers talking to a group about how Harding Icefield was the largest in the States—and almost twenty-three-thousand years old. "Our hikes up in the Rockies and Blue Ridge mountains pale in comparison to this."

"Yeah." Woody carefully secured their protein bar wrappers in one of the zippered pockets on his bag. The park had a strict policy of packing out all trash. "I'm glad we started here."

"Oh?" Eddie got slowly to his feet, reaching down to pull Woody up with him.

"Close to home. Learning a few lessons about hiking. It's not as terrifying as traveling halfway across the world." Woody took a swig of water, then handed the bottle over to Eddie. "Ready to head back?"

He took one last photo of the glacier stretching out in front of them. They'd upload the photos later using the laptop Estelle insisted they take. She'd download the images, allowing them to keep their memory cards clear for each step of the journey, mostly to stop him from ranting about the lack of security in the cloud storage. "Never imagined I'd see anything even close to this."

"Not in person," Woody agreed. They waved at a few hikers they'd met the day before on the *easy* trail. The four, from San Francisco, were part of a group that jokingly referred to itself as LPU—Loud, Proud, and Under A Cloud. They organized hikes around the world for the LGBTQIA community. "Y'all enjoying yourselves?"

"Dying." PJ had been the least enthused member of the group. They lay stretched out on the ground. "I think."

"They're fine." Meadow had her arm around her wife. They'd all been sitting on a blanket, having a picnic on a glacier. It was one item on the bucket list that they'd showed Eddie the night before. "Mostly. I think."

Abel, the only dude in the group, lifted his head up and waved cheerfully. "Where you two heading next?"

"We decided to backpack and camp along the Russian Lakes Trail. After y'alls advice, we're going to take our time. Do about ten miles a day, camp at night, and give ourselves at least a day to just explore the area. We already reserved a shuttle for the end of the trail to give us a ride back to our rental." Eddie was excited. He hadn't been camping in the woods for ages. They had better gear than he'd ever owned. They hoped to fish for their meals, though they'd gotten supplies just in case. "How about you four? Where to next?"

"Lost Lake Trail, maybe." PJ managed to pull themselves up and swiped bright green hair out of their face. "If it's lost, how can we hike it?"

"That joke? It wasn't funny the first twenty times

you told it," Abel grumbled. "Maybe we'll see you two in Anchorage or Fairbanks. We'll be up there for a few weeks."

Saying their goodbyes, Eddie followed Woody along the path toward the trail leading down from the Icefields. They'd been warned the last part of the circuit tended to go quickly but was also slippery. He had no intention of breaking a leg or twisting an ankle on the rocks.

Woody would *never* let him live it down if Eddie ruined the trip losing his footing on their first serious hike. They managed to shave off twenty minutes from the expected time and took time to stretch before getting into their rented SUV.

Meadow had texted them several videos of yoga and stretches. She claimed her wife, Vanessa, had almost done permanent damage after a long, strenuous hike. The following morning she'd been unable to move and required a lengthy visit with a hot bath and Epsom salts.

"We should make our own videos. Redneck hiking yoga." Woody grinned when Eddie glanced over his shoulder to find him staring at his ass. "Or maybe naked hiking yoga—and I'm the only one who gets to watch."

Eddie rolled his eyes and leaned against the side of the vehicle with a tired groan. "I'm starving."

"Fine. Dinner, first. Then I'll demonstrate how flexible I can be." Woody tossed him the keys. "Your turn to drive."

"Chinook?"

Woody held up his phone. "I got the directions from PJ last night."

The group of friends they'd met had sworn by a restaurant called Chinook. PJ, in particular, had raved about the scallop mac 'n' cheese and a s'mores pot du crème. Eddie had no idea what that was, but it sounded amazing.

"Steak, cheese, dessert."

"And duck tacos." Woody snickered.

"We are not getting the duck tacos. Because I know, through the entire meal, you are going to exclaim in your Donald Duck voice that they killed your family." Eddie didn't want to get thrown out of another restaurant because Woody had taken leave of his senses, again. "And no, you can't be Huey, Dewey, or Louie."

"What about Daffy?"

"No." Eddie sighed.

"My genius is never appreciated." Woody's phone loudly proclaimed they needed to take a left turn. "I've honed my craft over the years."

"Clearing your throat isn't a craft."

"See if I suck your dick again." Woody grinned at him. He set his phone in the cup holder and reached down for his camera. "I got a great photo of your ass in those jeans."

"I'm sure Essie will enjoy it immensely."

CHAPTER TEN

WOODY

ANOTHER SIX O'CLOCK WAKE-UP A DAY AFTER THEIR Icefield hike allowed them to get packed, eat breakfast, and drive out to where they'd be parking their rental. They intended to make the twenty-one-mile trail into a five-day trek. It gave them at least two days to explore the area around their campsite before hiking eleven miles to the next one.

The Russian Lakes Trail was a one-way route. They'd arranged with a local business to have a shuttle pick them up on the fifth day and drive them back to their vehicle. Woody couldn't contain his excitement; camping had always been one of his favorite ways to relax.

Camping.

Fishing.

Fucking in the forest.

Not necessarily in order of importance either.

Camping gear had been easy to rent in Seward. Woody wasn't sure how Estelle had organized everything so flawlessly from South Carolina. *Here's hoping she's a benevolent dictator when she takes over the world.*

"Let's get going." Eddie did one last walk around their cabin. They'd put some of their gear in storage at the lodge to allow room for the extra camping stuff. "Got the postcards?"

Woody collected the stack from the nightstand. "Stamped, addressed, and ready to drop in the mailbox we saw on the way to the trail."

Remembering his promise to his nieces, Woody had picked up a random selection of postcards in both Anchorage and Seward to send to the girls. Kat had explained how they wanted to create a mural on their bedroom walls with them. He made an effort to pick the prettiest ones available.

And a funny one with a bear in the woods for JJ.

The stack of postcards had grown to thirty when Eddie decided to get into the action and find one for his family. Woody hoped they didn't send this many at every stop on their journey. Maybe they could put all of them in an envelope to send to Estelle to distribute for them.

Nah, she'll skin us alive.

And she would.

After talking with the couple who ran the supply store, they'd opted to start on the south end of the trail. They'd suggested it over the north end for two reasons. It allowed them to immediately immerse themselves in the quiet and less crowded space, and the hike would include a lot more downhill than the other side.

And we are lazy sons of bitches.

The other tip had been to bring bear spray, bells,

and mosquito netting. Ten minutes into their hike, Woody had already swatted six mosquitos. His arm looked like a crime scene.

"How stupid would I look if I draped a mosquito net over me like a cape?" Woody asked when they stopped for a water and photo break. "Also, how many close-up photos of this squirrel's balls are too many?"

"Anything over ten." Eddie held a bag toward him. They'd picked up a bunch of salmon jerky sold by one of the local shops. "Time to trade off holding the kitchen supplies."

They'd rented a frying pan, pot, and bought a few food supplies. It would give them more options than trying to eat raw fish or salmon on a stick. *Man cannot live by fish alone.*

The store owner had also warned them about bears. Several times. Eddie had snickered behind Woody's back every single time. Woody threatened to spray him with the repellant if he didn't quit.

"Question."

Woody finished chewing on jerky and grabbed the bag of supplies. "What's the question?"

"Have you ever gone to third base in a lake?"

"What's a blowjob on the baseball scale of sex?" Woody followed Eddie down the trail. They had four more miles to go before they hit their first campsite of the hike. "Third?"

"Two balls and a strike."

He inhaled the small bite of jerky still in his mouth and wound up coughing until his eyes watered. "You're a dickhead."

Eddie reached back to grab Woody by the hand, dragging him forward. "Whoever catches the first fish gets the blowjob."

Kissing Eddie had become his favorite hobby. Woody briefly wondered what other hikers thought of two six-foot-something, broad-shouldered men making out in the middle of a trail in the Alaskan wilderness. Eddie's tongue slowly traced his lips, and he decided nothing else mattered.

Until a mosquito landed on his nose, Woody managed to hit both of them while trying to smack the bloodthirsty bug. Eddie scrambled to catch his hat and sunglasses. Woody took off down the trail, laughing and dodging the random bits of flora being flung at his back.

"Quit stoning me with branches."

"You knocked my sunglasses off," Eddie grumbled. "They landed in scat."

"Well, shit happens." Woody picked up his speed, which was hard when he couldn't stop snickering. "I'll buy you new ones."

"We're in the woods. For days."

Woody tried to keep out of reach, but the extra bag made it harder to dodge out of Eddie's reach. "Will you stop yanking on my shirt?"

Their bickering lasted another mile and a half. They arrived at their campsite for the next twenty-four hours a good thirty minutes ahead of time. Their long legs had carried them faster than the hiking estimates they'd seen online.

Of the two campsites around the Upper Russian Lake, one was open for them. They made quick work of setting up their tent, getting a fire going, and pulling out their supplies. Eddie stored their food in the storage box provided by the park for avoiding unwanted attention from bears.

As the sun slowly set across the lake, Woody enjoyed watching Eddie cooking up their dinner of fried potatoes and fish. The couple at the other campsite had caught an extra one and offered it to them. They'd also given them suggestions for the best places to explore in the morning.

Sitting under the stars, Woody enjoyed the crackling of their fire. They'd picked up enough deadfall to ensure warmth throughout the night, and so they'd stretched out on their backs on top of their sleeping bags. Even living out in the boondocks of South Carolina, he'd never seen such a magnificent night sky.

He wished his camera skills were up to the task of capturing the sight. "If you told me a month ago we'd be up here, I'd have thought you'd lost all of your marbles."

Eddie watched him in silence for a few seconds. His tongue slowly ran along his bottom lip, making Woody's dick twitch in his boxers with interest. *Is there anything sexier?*

Eddie grabbed Woody by the T-shirt. "Do you know how many times when we went camping in the backwoods that I wanted to strip you naked and enjoy every inch of your body?"

Woody had only a moment to be grateful for the distance between them and their camping neighbors before Eddie covered him like a defensive end on a quarterback. He grinned up at the intense brown eyes that were focused on him. "Well? What are you waiting for, Eddison?"

Teasing Eddie had never been a good idea. He tended to take things as a challenge. Woody found himself naked and on his stomach in the blink of an eye.

What would we do if a bear attacked now?

Fingers began to spread his thighs apart, tracing along the scar from an errant nail gun incident years ago.

I suppose you could say a bear is attacking me now.

"Think you can keep your mouth shut for more than a minute?"

"If all it takes is a minute, we've got bigger issues than my mouth." Woody didn't want the other hikers coming to check on them. He inhaled sharply when Eddie went from teasing to wrapping his fingers around Woody's dick and grinding himself against his behind. "Ed."

"Hush. I'm about to cross another item off our bucket list."

"Fucking by firelight?" Woody groaned as Eddie's strong fingers continued to stroke him. "Ah, hell."

"Not yet, we've got heaven to visit first," Eddie drawled.

They made love slowly. Under the Alaskan night sky. With an audience of mosquitos.

They'd done fast. They'd snuck in moments in an airplane and while driving. Hard and soft. They'd more than made up for all the time they'd lost by pretending they weren't in love and lust.

With stars and fire as their only light, Woody somehow found another level. Eddie timed his thrusts with a stroke of his fingers along Woody's shaft. Their bodies rose and fell together, finding a rhythm like the water lapping at the edge of the lake.

It took longer than a minute.

And when they'd finished, dragged themselves into the tent, and collapsed side by side on their backs, staring up at the dimly lit fabric overhead, Woody had one very important thing on his mind.

"A mosquito bit me in the butt."

"Sweet meat."

"Dickhead." Woody was too busy trying to catch his breath to fully respond. "You're rubbing cream on my mosquito bite."

"I think I already did that."

"*Dick. Head.*"

"Yep, with that."

Woody covered his face with one hand and reached down to scratch the offending bite. "Stop snickering at my pain."

"Pain in the ass."

"I hate you. And I hate mosquitos." Woody stretched his legs out, bumping the edge of the tent. "Mostly the bugs, though."

CHAPTER ELEVEN

EDDIE

Skinny dipping in an ice-cold lake in Alaska. Check.

Sex in the lake. Check.

Sex in the woods. Check.

Sex in the tent. Check

How many places to have sex on a bucket list are too many?

Camping had been a dream. They'd managed to avoid the occasionally temperamental September weather up until their last day. The rain started on their last mile out of the park and Eddie had never been more thankful to see the scruffy driver of their shuttle.

After picking up their stored items and returning the camping gear, they made the drive back to Anchorage for two nights in the same luxurious suite at the hotel. Amazing food. Plus an evening out at a dive bar with the eclectic group of hikers they'd met in Seward. Eddie had actually been sorry when they'd woken up on the third day to make the long drive to Fairbanks.

On advice from the hotel concierge, they'd mapped the slightly longer journey via Route One and Four. It would allow them to enjoy the beauty of driving through the Wrangell St. Elias Mountains. Not the fastest route, but apparently well worth the extra hour or two.

The rain had dropped the temperatures but brought beautiful blue skies for their journey. And yet another early morning wake-up. Eddie had taken the first leg of the drive. Woody had snored for a good hour before Eddie punched him in the leg.

"What?"

"Sun's up."

Autumn in Alaska seemed to be all jewel-toned bronze and golden. The rising sun glinting off the trees and lake dazzled him when contrasted with the stark gray mountains capped off with glistening snow. He could readily understand how so many artists had been inspired by the landscape.

"Fairbanks or bust?" Woody sat up in the passenger seat. He reached down to grab the bag of snacks they'd picked up the night before. "Salty or sweet?"

"Salty." Eddie grinned wickedly. "Any meat left?"

Woody grabbed his crotch and winked at him. "Got a stick right here."

"How about jerky?"

"I'll—"

"Yes, I know. I mean actual food I can chew. I'm starving." Eddie thought he deserved a medal for resisting the urge to pull over to the side of the road and have a little fun. He didn't think the state troopers would be amused, but Woody playing with himself through his jeans made it difficult. "Mothertrucker. Will you quit that?"

"Fine. Reindeer, beef, or salmon?" Woody dug through the various items in the grocery bag. He pulled out a six-pack of chocolate donuts and set them on the dashboard. "Here. Try the reindeer."

"On Dasher."

"Santa's going to send you coal this year." Woody pried open the bag and held it out to him. "Want some of my meat?"

"Linwood," Eddie growled when Woody kept pulling jerky out of reach. "Don't make me turn this car around."

He gave a full-body shudder. "I'm having a flashback to being stuck in the station wagon as a kid on a road trip to Houston."

"That the one where you got in trouble for trying to sell JJ to the circus?"

Their drive took an hour longer than intended. Eddie blamed Woody for his wanting to stop every thirty minutes to take a photo. Woody argued it was his own fault for deciding they should pull over for a blowjob to avoid crashing.

Semantics.

After checking into their hotel, they'd rushed across Fairbanks to get to the Pump House for dinner. PJ had promised them the place had fascinating menu options. The reindeer meatballs on the menu had definitely caught their attention.

Woody had ordered them mostly, Eddie knew, because he wanted to be able to say he'd eaten reindeer balls for an appetizer. They were consistent in their inability to be serious for long periods of time. They also tried the elk sliders.

And elk meatloaf.

"Elk meatloaf," Eddie repeated for the fifth time.

He'd eaten game before. They lived in rural South Carolina. He'd tried deer, squirrel, and even alligator. Elk meatloaf struck him as pedestrian and extraordinary at the same time.

Woody stole a bite of it. "Best meatloaf I've tried."

"Don't tell Mama Ester." Eddie made the sign of the cross to ward off evil. "She'll hunt us down."

"And force-feed us her meatloaf."

The meal left both of them feeling overly stuffed. Eddie was grateful they wouldn't have a hike the next morning. He thought he'd be more likely to crawl along the trail rather than walk.

The following day, they moved from their hotel to the Borealis Base Camp. Estelle had managed, somehow, to book several nights in one of their guest domes. It would allow them to sleep under the stars and the northern lights for several days.

We can fuck under the northern lights without freezing our balls off.

Another check on my bucket list.

The dome made Eddie think of a fiberglass igloo with a massive window overhead. They'd stayed in bed the first night and stared at the northern lights in awe. Eddie had always dreamed of seeing them; it had been more than he ever imagined.

"Like a brushstroke of glitter across the sky." Eddie

remembered vividly how his mom had described the aurora borealis. She'd seen them once many years ago. "Not sure a photo or video will do this justice."

The shimmering green light across the sky had been difficult to capture. Eddie had tried. Woody hadn't bothered, since they'd bought a few prints from a local photographer who did know what he was doing.

And we definitely don't.

Eddie scrolled through the images on his camera, deleting almost all of his attempts to photograph the lights. He set the camera aside and lay back to stare up again at the night sky. "Not sure how I feel about the existence of god most days, but there's a magic to this place."

Woody shifted closer to him. "Why didn't we ever do this before?"

"Travel to Alaska and throw money around like we're swimming in it?"

Woody didn't answer for several minutes. Long enough that Eddie glanced over to see if he'd fallen asleep. He eventually continued with his thought. "Be together."

"Fear." Eddie went for the truth instead of a glib, humorous response. "Fear of throwing away our friendship. Fear of how our families and neighbors might respond. Fear of screwing up a good thing."

"You weren't in the closet, though. Neither was I." Woody shifted closer until their sides were pressed together. He dropped a hand onto Eddie's thigh. "Why didn't we try?"

"How much more time are you going to waste

thinking about what-ifs? We *did* finally get here, right?" Eddie frowned at Woody. If he had any pet peeves, it was Woody's tendency to beat himself up over mistakes. "Got a time machine?"

"No."

"Then get over it already." Eddie reached down to cover the hand on his thigh. "And enjoy the northern lights."

"You enjoy the northern lights." Woody moved onto his knees and shifted down the mattress. "Is a blowjob under the stars on your bucket list?"

"It is now."

Check.

CHAPTER TWELVE

WOODY

"If you don't quit laughing, I swear I'm gonna kick your butt," Eddie snapped. He sat on a tree stump in front of their rental vehicle while pulling off his boots and socks. "Woody."

He tried valiantly not to laugh, even clamping his mouth shut and practically wheezing in an effort not to chuckle. "How'd you like dog sledding?"

"So help me."

Their last Alaska bucket list item had been dog sledding. Day one had gone well. The second had ended with one of the beautiful huskies deciding to show them who the true alpha was.

Woody successfully dodged the stream of pee.

Eddie hadn't.

Woody was laughing.

Eddie definitely wasn't.

"You can kiss my grass." Eddie threw his sock at Woody, who easily dodged out of the way. "And you're buying me new hiking boots."

"We went to Alaska, and all we got was pee-soaked socks." He glanced over at Eddie, and they both collapsed in a fit of laughter. "Maybe we won't write home about this part of our trip."

Laughter always brought out the best in Eddie. Woody remembered being mesmerized by his best friend's laugh in high school like it was yesterday. His spirit seemed to shine through always.

"Ed."

"Wood."

"Ed." Woody grinned at his best friend. "Let's get back to the hotel before you get frostbite on your toes."

The socks and shoes went in the trash. Eddie had a thing about cleanliness, and even multiple trips through a washing machine wouldn't have been enough. Woody did snap a quick photo of them; even the not-so-perfect moments of their journey should be remembered.

Before they left Fairbanks, Woody insisted on stopping at Mrs. Claws, a chocolate shop. He wanted to ship out several boxes. Estelle, Mama Ester, and Kat would all greatly appreciate his thoughtfulness.

He bought three bars of the bacon chocolate mousse crunch. It lasted not even an hour into their drive back to Anchorage. They'd chosen a different, faster route for their last road trip before catching their flight to Montana.

The weeks in Alaska had flown by. Woody was grateful Estelle insisted on them getting cameras. He didn't know if he'd even remember half of what they'd done without photographic evidence; they'd managed to cram in a lot of hiking and food into less than a month.

And now they intended to fly from Alaska to Montana with a brief layover in Portland. They'd been sitting in the airport for three hours waiting for their flight to arrive. The weather had kept it grounded in Oregon, which meant they'd miss their connecting flight.

"When are you coming home, Uncle Woody?" Kitty yelled over her dad's voice on the phone. "Don't forget my postcards."

Before Woody could respond, he heard Kat corralling her giggling daughters out of the room. He'd chosen to pass the time by calling his brother. A few seats down, Eddie was having a quiet conversation with his parents, who were pressing him for details about their trip.

Well, it isn't exactly about the trip.

They appeared to be harassing him for gossip about their relationship. Woody grinned when Eddie glared at him. Parental pressure could be hard to resist.

And Edna Howard knew how to play dirty.

When they were teens, Edna had always been the one to get confessions out of them. She tended to be the most understanding. Her punishments were doled out with a serving of cookies.

Cookies that tasted so good his mouth watered even now, however many years later. They'd eaten in five-star restaurants, but Edna and Mama Ester made food to feed the body and soul. He wondered if they had time to make a pit stop in South Carolina.

Turning his attention back to his brother, Woody promised JJ they'd stop by home for a few days. They'd be finished in Montana and Canada, the last legs of their trip before they'd head south to Peru, in a few weeks. They could afford to visit with family for a bit.

After ending the call with his brother, Woody wandered over to check on their flight. Still delayed. They had no idea when a plane would be available. He wondered if they could drive from Anchorage to the Glacier National Park faster than flying at this point.

Scanning the departing flights not delayed, Woody spotted one leaving for Seattle in less than an hour. *Perfect.* With a little drawl of southern charm, he managed to get their tickets (and luggage) switched. A text to Estelle had her scrambling to get their rental car changed to their new destination.

Seattle to their hotel in West Glacier, Montana, would be a relatively easy nine-hour drive. They'd even get to travel through several national forests, a bonus in his opinion. He'd enjoy it more than waiting endlessly at an airport.

"Change of plans." Woody grabbed Eddie, dragging him out of his chair and dragging him toward their new gate. "We're flying to Seattle."

"We are?" Eddie had already hung up with his parents and slipped his phone into his pocket. "Why?"

"Would you rather sit in the airport for three more hours, or fly to Seattle and drive to Montana?" Woody knew both of them would enjoy a road trip more than flying, even if the journey took longer. "Eh?"

Eddie shoved him slightly. "You're not nice enough to be Canadian. And your accent is crap."

"Eh?"

Their new flight left on time. They arrived in Seattle, picked up their shiny SUV rental, and managed to swing by Mighty O's for two dozen donuts and large coffees. JJ did not appreciate his texting a photo with a mouthful of chocolate raspberry pastry, if the expletive response was anything to go by.

He hadn't known his brother could be so creative.

Twenty-four donuts and two large coffees carried them through four hours of their drive. Woody had no regrets. They expected to crash from the sugar and caffeine rush eventually.

And it happened around mile two hundred and fifty.

They hit a wall, one built of sugar and waking up early in the morning for days on end. Eddie was the one to make the decision to stop in Spokane. After speaking with Estelle, they drove into the city to the Davenport Grand Hotel.

As Eddie had pointed out, the trip was all about their enjoyment. If they wanted to stop for a few days in a different city, who cared? They had the money and nothing pushing them.

They'd discovered money opened a lot of doors, a privilege they tried to appreciate rather than simply take advantage of. Woody certainly wasn't going to complain when they fell backward onto the plush king mattress of the Presidential suite of the hotel.

"We have to move." Woody nudged Eddie with his elbow six hours later, after their impromptu nap. "I'm hungry."

"We ate our weight in donuts."

"Seven hours ago." Woody continued perusing the

dinner suggestions the concierge had left for them. "There's a restaurant called The Flying Goat."

"I'm awake." Eddie sat up and leaned over to look at the image on Woody's phone. "The Flying Goat. Think they serve goat?"

"It'll be a culinary adventure."

"You're not allowed to watch the Food Network again. You're not Bobby Flay." He rolled himself off the bed onto his feet, stretching his tall frame and giving Woody a great view of his abdomen as his shirt rose up. "Don't even think about it. I need something other than sugar before we do anything else."

They took advantage of the car service the hotel offered, allowing them to try several of the craft beers offered at the restaurant. Woody had already made a list for himself of the ones he wanted to get a taste of. He wasn't sure any of them went with goat, but maybe the name was just that—a name.

Turned out to just be a name.

Woody didn't know if he was relieved or disappointed; goat pizza would've made for an interesting experience. Their journey had been all about stepping outside of their comfort zones. "We're trying the pickled egg."

"Why?"

"Because it's there." Woody grinned at the resigned frown on Eddie's face. "What pizzas are we getting?"

Unable to pick one each, they'd ordered four. Woody found he preferred the pulled pork and onion pizza with the sweet and tart honey apple BBQ sauce. He'd fought Eddie for the last slice.

Hand on heart the best damn pizza I've ever eaten. I wonder if they'd sell me a gallon bucket of the sauce.

I could shower in it.

Eddie could shower in it, and I could lick it off him.

Good plan.

"Whatever you're thinking, no." Eddie pointed a finger at him. "I know that look. We got suspended from the varsity team because of it."

"Well, bless my soul." Woody put his hand on his chest, doing a fair impression of a shocked Mama Ester. "I'll pray for you."

"Dickhead."

The meal ended as most did, with them in laughter and heavy petting under the table where the server couldn't see. They stumbled toward their ride drunk on food and one beer too many. Woody made sure to leave an extra nice tip for the server and also their driver, partly because it was hard to pay attention to dollar amounts when Eddie's tongue was teasing along his neck and earlobe.

"Did we have to give the driver a show?"

"Highlight of his night." Eddie had a tight grasp on his hand, dragging him into the elevator.

"The highlight of his night was the tip."

"A tip is going to be *more* than a highlight of your night." Eddie went back to paying close attention to the sensitive spot on Woody's neck with his lips and tongue. "Is pickled egg an aphrodisiac?"

"No, but I'm not sure I'll ever recover from hearing pickled egg called an aphrodisiac." Woody started to laugh, only to have it swallowed up in a moan when

Eddie slid his fingers straight down to the front of his jeans. "Damn."

"Ready for dessert?" Eddie teased.

Deciding not to mention his sudden urge for sweet and tart honey apple BBQ sauce, Woody darted out of the elevator and fumbled with the door to their presidential suite. Eddie followed, casually stripping off his clothes and flinging them to the side as he went. They'd both toed off their sneakers almost immediately upon entering the room.

"Heads or tails?" Woody dug a quarter out of his jeans pocket.

Flipping a coin had started as a joke in their tent. Woody hadn't been able to decide what he wanted to do. Heads or tails seemed an obvious and hilarious option.

Eddie knocked the quarter out of his hand and shoved him onto the bed.

Tails it is.

Woody rested his head against one of the oversized pillows and watched Eddie impatiently yank on his jeans. "Want me to—"

"Shut your mouth." Eddie managed to get them off without Woody helping. "Do you know how many times I dreamed about you sprawled out naked in front of me?"

"You'll get tired of it eventually."

Waving off the comment, Eddie crawled onto the bed. He caught Woody by the arm, flipping him over onto his stomach and lifting his hips slightly. They moved together with the casual fluidity of a couple who'd been together for years—not months.

It's going to be a damn good night.

And it was.

Eddie, always the more patient between them, took his time. He grabbed the lube from the nightstand; Woody hadn't even known the bottle was there. Eddie's fingers drove any thought about it completely out of his mind.

He wanted to beg for more.

He wouldn't.

Woody could hear a teasing Eddie in his mind singing "Ain't too proud to beg," except he was.

For all their earlier exhaustion, Woody found the energy to meet Eddie thrust for thrust. Round one ended on the bed, while round two moved into the living area with their beautiful view of Spokane from the floor-to-ceiling windows. They languidly made love until they collapsed on the soft couch, completely spent.

"Hey," Woody managed after several minutes of staring out the window. "You owe me a quarter."

"Bill me."

CHAPTER THIRTEEN

EDDIE

"Think we ordered too much?" Eddie surveyed the multiple plates covering their small table at Frank's Diner. They hadn't been able to pick one meal each, so they'd ordered a variety. "Can we even eat all this?"

"Watch me." Woody dug into his sirloin eggs benedict enthusiastically. "Want some?"

"Of course."

Sharing their way through waffles, biscuits and gravy, a bacon, sausage, and gruyere omelet, and the sirloin benedict, Eddie didn't know how he hadn't gained twenty pounds in one meal. It was definitely worth it, even if he wanted to nap for a year. They dragged themselves outside to squeeze into the SUV with full groans.

They stopped on the way out of the city to get gas and two Spokane postcards for Woody's nieces. Eddie knew Woody would never break his promise to the little girls. They'd get mail from every city.

They took the scenic route north of Spokane

through the Kaniksu National Forest, pausing for photos a few times. They mooned a squirrel. He appreciated the view.

So did Eddie. He always enjoyed watching Woody from behind, in or out of his jeans.

"This cottage is…." Woody stood outside of their cabin at the Belton Chalet on the edge of Glacier National Park.

"Something your momma would stay at." Eddie stared around the cute cottage. It was nice, but after fancy hotel rooms and tents, almost disconcerting. "Think we can squeeze into the claw-foot tub together?"

"Only if you want to use WD-40 to squeeze ourselves out of it." Woody had been fascinated by it when they did the walkthrough of the cottage. "We'll have to keep the curtains closed, or our neighbors will get quite a view."

"No sex on the lawn." Eddie snickered.

The cottage didn't feel comfortable. Granted, neither had the presidential suite. But the sweet little cabin made Eddie feel like he was on someone else's honeymoon or family vacation.

"It's like the Baptist summer camp all over again." Woody sat on the steps of the cottage. "I'm having flashbacks."

"Which year?"

"Chastity camp."

Eddie didn't even bother trying to hide his laughter. "Oh, right. The year I sent you a box of porn magazines. You never said thanks."

"They screened the mail." Woody leaned back on

the stairs, holding his side while he laughed. "Can you imagine the look on their faces?"

"So, what're we doing?"

Woody tilted his head to stare at him. "Not sleeping in there."

All right.

We're not sleeping in the cabin.

"Need a moment?" Eddie's grin turned into a frown. He knew Woody played off some of his issues with his family, but there were definitely lingering scars. "You enjoy the sunlight. I'll see if Estelle can work her magic."

Wandering away from the cottages, Eddie found a little privacy out of earshot of Woody. His cousin had a soft spot for him. He knew she'd move mountains to help put Woody at ease without making a big deal to embarrass him.

"Essie."

"No." Estelle didn't even wait to hear anything other than her name. "I'm busy."

"It's Woody."

As Eddie had assumed, Estelle immediately moved to try to finagle a last-minute room somewhere else. She found a cabin not far from them. They didn't bother trying to get a refund.

Only half listening to his cousin, Eddie kept an eye on Woody. *My best friend. Boyfriend? Everything? Quit sounding like one of Mama's favorite movies.* His family had surrounded Woody many times over the years with love; a new hotel was next to nothing in comparison.

"You coming?" Eddie nudged Woody's leg with his

foot, causing him to sit up and open his eyes. "Essie managed to find a hotel a few miles down the road. Oh, and I found your quarter."

Woody caught the coin flipped over to him. He glanced down at it then leered up at Eddie. "Heads."

"You're hornier than a…." Eddie scratched his jaw, unable to find the perfect comparison.

Woody pushed himself off the step, pocketing the coin and grabbing his bag. "Hornier than an old billy goat."

"Now you sound like my uncle Horace."

"And there goes the head. Dying a painful death thanks to my vivid imagination."

Their new cabin proved to be less traumatic for Woody. They dropped off their bags and immediately headed out to explore. They spent two weeks hiking the multiple trails on the Montana side of Glacier National Park.

Their last stop on the first leg of their world hiking tour was Banff National Park in Canada. Eddie had always wanted to trek through the Plain of Six Glaciers. The weather looked favorable when they checked into Chateau Lake Louise.

Their suite offered a spectacular view across both the lake and the Victoria Glacier. It had two private balconies. They'd already flipped a coin over which one they'd be getting naked on first.

Sex. In the freezing cold under the stars while looking across a glacier. We're living a very strange version of my daydreams about winning the lottery.

Over the course of two weeks, they slogged through

every day hike within driving distance. First, they'd done the easier strolls, starting with a casual walk around the river to see Bow River Falls. Fenland Trail also proved equally laid-back.

Healy Pass had been their longest and hardest hike. Eddie had loved every minute of it. The sweeping view of fall colors across the Great Divide would stick with him for a long while.

Gold leaves. Jagged white-capped mountains. Blue skies. The bronze meadow with glints from the sun bouncing off the shimmering lake. If Eddie had been a poet, he thought Healy Pass would easily have inspired a masterpiece.

While having a snack at the highest point of the trail, they'd run into a couple from LPU, the gay hiking group. They'd walked the rest of the way together, enjoying the company. Noah and Theo Chen worked with plants.

Eddie wasn't sure what that meant.

But Noah was apparently obsessed with plants and flowers, the more scientific of the two. He spent the entire hike pointing out various species of flora, much to his husband's amusement. They kept arguing about Noah wanting to take samples.

Tonight was their last night in Canada. Their flight left for home in the morning. Eddie and Woody invited their new friends to join them for a farewell dinner at Walliser Stube. Woody wanted to try the fondue.

Finishing up their hike, the group split up to shower and relax before dinner. Woody napped while Eddie responded to emails from his cousins running his gas station. They'd done an amazing job so far but screwed up on ordering inventory.

Eddie had to laugh. The first time he'd ordered inventory for the station, he'd wound up with twenty extra boxes of Twinkies and no toilet paper for the restrooms. Even after working with his parents at the diner, he'd gone through a lot of trial and error in being a business owner.

"How are they doing?" Woody rolled over to look at the tablet screen.

"They thought they'd requested a box of Twizzlers."

"And?"

"They ordered a pallet." Eddie enlarged the photo. He met Woody's gaze, and they both cracked up laughing. "I told them to keep a couple boxes for the station and donate the rest to the school. No way in hell they'll sell that many Twizzlers."

"I'll buy a box." Woody had an unhealthy obsession with candy of all sorts.

"Do you need a box of Twizzlers?"

"Yes." Woody rolled over onto his other side to grab his phone. "I'll text 'em."

"You have issues." Eddie shook his head in disbelief. "We're traveling the world, and you want a million rubber straws."

"Never insult the Twizzler."

"Issues. Many. Many. Issues." Eddie finished up his own message to his cousins. "We've got ten minutes to get to the restaurant for fondue."

When Eddie had imagined fondue, he'd thought about the gunky, greasy attempt they'd made once in college. It had seemed easy enough, but they'd been sick for days.

Walliser Stube didn't go in for gunk or grease.

Their meal started with a melt-in-your-mouth short rib, followed up with a cheese fondue seasoned with truffle, garlic, and mushroom. They had a mixture of vegetables and tender steak to dip into the liquid gold. Their dark chocolate dessert pot had been seasoned with Grand Marnier; Eddie could've licked the bowl clean, or taken it back to the room to cover a naked Woody.

And lick it off him.

"Can I get anything else for you gentlemen?"

Eddie grinned wickedly at the server. "Can I get some of the chocolate fondue to go?"

CHAPTER FOURTEEN

WOODY

HOME.

Sleeping alone hadn't gone well. Woody tossed and turned until three in the morning the first night home. Eddie snuck into his bed at four, and then they were both dead to the world until reality woke them at eight.

"I'll get it." Woody stumbled out of bed to answer the furious knocking. He barely managed to get a T-shirt and sweatpants on before opening the door. "What do you want? Hell. How'd you even know I was here?"

"Linwood." His mother had on her Sunday best. She smelled like she had bathed in honeysuckle. He rubbed his nose to fend off a sneeze. "We love you. We've missed you."

You love that I have money.

And you want some of it.

Missed me?

Breathe, man, breathe.

"Lord have mercy." His dad grabbed his mom and

yanked her away from the door. "What the devil has gotten into you?"

Woody glanced in confusion over his shoulder, only to choke on his tongue when he found a naked Eddie standing there in all his morning glory. "You definitely had clothes on a second ago."

Eddie made a show of flexing his muscles. He stepped up behind Woody, resting his arm on Woody's shoulder as they watched the Robinsons rush away. "Was it something I said? Think they'll pray for us?"

"What're you doing?" Woody kicked his door shut and allowed Eddie to guide him back through the house to the bedroom. "Ed?"

"Tired of their horseshit." Eddie kissed him roughly, then threw himself on the bed with a groan. "I need another hour before I face the world. I'm not letting them run all over you."

"And you naked was the solution?"

"It worked." Eddie didn't show any signs of remorse. "How long before someone else invades our quiet morning?"

"Considering we're only here for a few days? Not long." Woody aborted his move to lean in for a kiss when they heard the door opening and twin giggles. "Put some damn clothes on before they barge in here."

Making his way out of the room, Woody shut the door behind him. He caught his nieces, who launched themselves at him in the hallway. They giggled all the way into the living room, where JJ was lounging on the sofa with a cup of coffee.

"Comfortable?" Woody dumped one of his nieces on his brother's shoulder. "You're up early."

"They wanted to see Uncle Woody before school." JJ checked his watch and got to his feet with a muffled curse. "And now they're going to be late."

Their two days in South Carolina flew by in a flurry of laundry, checking in with family, and avoiding old friends who suddenly wanted to reacquaint themselves. Woody discovered a handful of new cousins he'd never met. Or heard of. He'd heard tragic stories worthy of a singing competition on the TV.

Their children needed help paying for medical procedures. When Woody pressed them, the details of their story always seemed to fall apart. He sent a thank-you text to Judge for helping to handle their winnings.

How much of a nightmare would this all be if everyone knew we'd won?

Gossip had carried the story far enough as it was. Estelle had been a genius to get them out of town within days of collecting their winnings. Out of sight, out of mind. The story would eventually fade.

Though Woody supposed they'd be hunted by the more persistent. His parents immediately sprung to mind. He doubted even a protection order would keep them away.

Despite their shock at Eddie's nakedness, they still managed to send multiple emails to Woody. Passive-aggressive notes encouraging him to mend his ways, which seemed to mostly involve giving them a large chunk of his newfound wealth. Thankfully, they'd leave for Peru in the morning, the first stop on the next leg of their journey

Estelle had organized their time for the next three months down to the minute. November would be spent in Peru, Chile, and Easter Island. Around December, they'd move to Bolivia, Uruguay, and finish up their South American adventure in Paraguay.

After a family dinner with the Howards, they'd driven out to Columbia to visit the hiking store and caught up with their young friend, Sharon. She added a few items to their gear, given their plans to hike in the Cordillera Blanca. They planned to do a lot of trekking —new shoes had been a must as well.

A few days later, after three plane rides and an eight-hour journey in a bus that ended in a near-death experience, Woody and Eddie had made their first steps on a ten-day hike along the Huayhuash circuit. Their insane drive from Lima to Huaraz had given them a beautiful view of Cordillera Blanca. Worth the scenery, even if they'd feared for their lives a few times.

Three days in Huaraz allowed them to explore the area and acclimatize themselves to the high altitude. On advice from Abel, who they'd met in Seward, they'd booked a guided hike through Huayhuash through Quechuandes, a highly recommended trekking company that provided both a guide, a cook, and pack animals. Their friends from LPU had suggested going it alone could be especially dangerous at the start of the rainy season.

"Are we ready for this?" Woody tugged on a knit hat. They'd exchanged their usual ball caps for beanies to keep warm, given the cool temperatures they expected, particularly in the evenings. "Ten days hiking over passes through one of the best hiking trails in the world?"

"Piece of cake."

Eddie

"Twizzler?"

Eddie snagged two from the bag Woody held out to him. "What's the nutritional value of a Twizzler?"

Woody shrugged with a stick of licorice dangling from his mouth like a cigarette. "Less than cum, more than a piece of gum."

Eddie had to spit out the food in his mouth to keep from choking. He fell off the rock, laughing so hard tears poured from his eyes. "Damn it, Wood."

"Wood usually is involved."

"Stop," Eddie wheezed. He rolled over on his side and got back up on the rock. "I can't breathe."

The mountains stretched out in a jagged line in the distance. Today was one of their three rest days. They'd opted not to take part in any extra climbing, instead enjoying their campsite by one of the lakes in the valley; they'd even taken a dip in the freezing water.

Cannonballing into the water had been a shock to the system. Their guide had laughed at Woody's expense when Eddie dragged him into the lake. It was definitely the most interesting swim Eddie had ever done.

Daniel, their guide, had led them through their first days and passes. Eddie was glad, given the terrain, that they'd opted for hiring a professional. For one thing, they didn't have to carry food for ten days on their backs.

Their LPU friends had warned them against overt public displays of affection. Rural communities in Peru weren't always open-minded. Woody had, of course, taken that as a challenge to be covert about it.

Sex high above sea level? Check.

"How's your butt cheek?"

"Dude." Woody waved a half-eaten Twizzler at him. "Don't start."

"You had to cannonball one last time." Eddie snickered.

During their dip in the lake, Woody had managed to scrape his butt against the rocks. It had been one of the reasons they'd opted for a more relaxed rest day. Eddie had been kind enough to not tease him too much.

"Rain's coming in." Woody changed the subject, making Eddie chuckle. "Think we'll be all right?"

"Should be. Just a little rain."

Other hikers had warned them November could be a tricky time of year for hiking, though not as bad as December or January. The weather up until today had been absolutely perfect. Blue skies, not hot but not freezing cold while the sun was out. Eddie hoped the trend continued and the ominous darkening sky didn't last long.

Turning away from the dark skies behind him, Eddie looked out across the mountains in front, watching ribbons of gray clouds roll across the peaks. The wind had definitely picked up. It whistled through the valley, whipping through the tall, dry grass and their tents down on the plateau.

"Ah, the sounds of the mountains. Wind, birds, and goats." Woody nodded toward a farmer on horseback who was guiding his herd along a path. They'd set up camp about two hours' walk from a village. "Clouds are settling in."

Over the course of an hour, they watched the clouds slowly sink down until the mountains were completely obscured. Rain began softly at first before beginning to pelt them mercilessly. They took shelter in their tents to ride out the first storm of the rainy season.

Their rest day turned into a hiding-in-the-tent sort of afternoon. The rain finally stopped in the evening, allowing the cook to fix up a meal for them, their guide, and the donkey handlers. Eddie had retained enough Spanish learned from his mom and Mama Ester to communicate with them, more than Woody, whose accented attempts had proved more amusing than useful.

He tried.

It was adorable. And hilarious. Eddie had to give their Peruvian guide props for not simply laughing in his face. He hadn't been capable of such restraint.

They made themselves comfortable in their sleeping bags. The following morning would take them through one of the hardest days of their trek. Eddie was looking forward to the adventure—and the hot springs.

Their next camp would be set up next to hot springs.

Eddie planned to spend at least an hour soaking. He hoped they remembered to take photos of their "spa day" for Estelle.

She'd probably accuse them of glamping.

"Ed?"

Eddie rolled over in his sleeping bag to find Woody peering intently down at the map of their trail. "Hmm?"

"Scale of one to ten. How damned amazing is our life?" Woody traced the lines on the map with his finger. "We're in the middle of the mountains in Peru."

"You don't get bonus points for stating the obvious." Eddie shifted closer, so they faced each other with the map between them. "Finally sinking in?"

Woody nodded absently. "Never thought I'd win more than a few bucks here or there."

"If you need convincing, remember your folks keep voluntarily trying to talk to you." Eddie brought his hand up to block the map when Woody went to whack him over the head with it. "Think the novelty of us being rich will wear off eventually? Not sure we'll be able to relax at home with people always wanting something from us."

"We could move."

"What about your family? And JJ, Kat, and the girls?" Woody folded up the map and slipped it into the front pocket of his backpack. He lay down, stretching out next to Eddie and resting his head on Eddie's pillow so their foreheads rested against one another. "We could move all of them."

"Move where? The moon?" Eddie didn't think leaving the city or even the state would be much of a deterrent for long. Money tended to mess with people's heads. "A problem for another day?"

"Why put off until tomorrow what we can deal with next year?" Woody tilted his head slightly until their lips met. "Tea ammo."

Eddie tried valiantly not to laugh. "Te amo?"

"That's what I said."

Eddie rolled over on his back and gave in to the urge to snicker. "I love you too."

Their extended hike in Peru had been magical, even if Eddie felt silly for using the word. Rainbows and unicorns, as Woody's nieces would say. They'd taken the terrifying bus ride back to Lima, then flown to Santiago, Chile.

Estelle had accurately predicted a need for a few days of rest. Several nights in the Presidential Suite at the Ritz-Carlton worked perfectly. They got their laundry taken care of and relaxed after the strenuous hike across the Huayhuash circuit.

He wasn't complaining.

The Presidential Suite felt more like a well-furnished New York penthouse apartment. Woody and Eddie planned to take advantage of the massive tub in the bathroom. They wanted to relax before heading out to enjoy a night out in Santiago.

"Water's getting cold."

"I doubt it." Eddie wandered into the bathroom, tossing his shirt to the side. He frowned at the tub, which seemed smaller with Woody already inside. "If we get stuck and have to call for help…."

"We're going to be jammed up for a while, because

unless you stuck your phone where the sun don't shine, we don't have a way to call for help." Woody shifted in the water, sloshing it over the side. "Get your butt in here. I want to see what sex next to the water jets is like."

"Of course you do."

Getting in the tub took some work. Eddie flailed for a second when his foot almost went out from underneath him. He managed to squeeze in across from Woody.

"Twist around this way between my legs. Isn't that how things work in romantic movies?" Woody grabbed him by the calf and tugged. "Ed."

He tried.

Eddie managed to shift around, only to get his right leg stuck underneath Woody's left thigh. "Crud muffin."

Woody threw his hand out to stop Eddie from crashing onto his chest. He slipped down in the tub under the weight. He moved to the right to avoid bashing his head on the tap. "Shit."

Telling himself not to laugh, Eddie had to tilt his chin up to catch his breath. He didn't want to inhale sudsy water. Every time he moved to lift himself up off Woody, he slipped on the slick sides of the tub.

"Fuck me."

"Not sure I can." Eddie laughed, then spluttered when Woody managed to splash him in the face. He considered their options. He didn't quite know how his limbs had gotten stuck wrapped around Woody. "This looks way easier in those movies my mama watches."

"Okay. I'm going to try to get out from under you

while you get on your knees." Woody shifted underneath him, and Eddie went face-first into the water. "Bad plan."

It took ten minutes of struggling and gasping for air from their raucous amusement at the slick, watery predicament. They finally managed to get out of the tub and collapsed on the marble surface. Suds covered their bodies and the floor.

"I feel relaxed." Eddie blinked up at the ceiling. "Should've stuck with the shower. Or the bed. Our six-foot-plus frames weren't meant for tub thumping."

"I need a hot dog."

"I was trying to give you one." Eddie stretched his back out, trying to make sure he hadn't twisted it. "Quit snickering."

On the ride from the airport to the hotel, Woody had tried to get an idea for what to eat in Santiago, with a little help from Eddie's ability to speak Spanish. They'd learned in Seward that asking locals, especially drivers and hotel staff, garnered them the best restaurants. They'd learned hot dogs were practically a must for most Chileans.

Hogs had immediately become their number one choice, if only because of the name of the restaurant. They'd checked out the menu online and been convinced. *Have you lived until you've tried a boar hot dog?*

Definitely not.

Eddie forced himself to his feet. His stomach had already started grumbling. "Dinner?"

"Dinner."

CHAPTER FIFTEEN

THREE BREAD OPTIONS.

Seven types of hot dogs.

Twenty kinds of toppings.

It felt like a challenge.

Of all the combinations, the boar dog with the Tex toppings wound up being his favorite. Melted buttery cheese, BBQ sauce, and crispy bacon. Woody had taken photos in the hopes of being able to recreate the magic. They had no regrets aside from having to roll themselves out of Hogs.

Completely stuffed, they did manage to make it to the waiting shuttle outside. Woody had asked Estelle to plan a unique experience for their visit since they would only be in Santiago for two full days. She'd found an evening tour at a private observatory in the mountains outside of the city.

Stargazing had always been something they enjoyed. Even at home in South Carolina, they'd often sit in his backyard by the fire pit to enjoy the night sky. Eddie had even talked about building his own telescope at one point.

The forty-minute drive from the city took them up into the Andes to a private observatory. For four hours they moved amidst a variety of telescopes lined up side by side to view the stars in a way they'd never seen. Woody sat back to watch Eddie, who was completely enthralled by the majesty overhead.

Woody drank wine, ignored the appetizer because his stomach was full to bursting, and enjoyed the pure joy on Eddie's face. *We came to the game of love late. But I think we're going to win.*

Eddie glanced over his shoulder, grinning at Woody. "Check this out."

I am in so much trouble.

Good trouble.

So much trouble.

Damn, his ass looks good in those jeans.

Stargazing had become one of their favorite downtime activities so far on their long adventure. Woody had even found an app for his phone with star charts. The longer their travels went, the more the complete change in their reality began to sink in.

The astronomer who owned the observatory had been so charmed by their genuine enthusiasm that their private tour went on for an additional hour. Woody wasn't wound up on the fancy snacks or wine. He did love watching Eddie throw himself into learning everything he could.

Given the late hour, they talked their driver into taking them to his favorite street vendor. *Sausage for every-*

one. Again. After another round of hot dogs, they climbed into bed to prepare for their early morning flight. They barely had the energy to strip down to their boxers; Eddie was snoring before Woody even got into the bed.

Woody slipped under the blanket and watched Eddie sleep for a while. His heart had always skipped a beat when he looked at the man beside him. *Love, man. Love.*

A five-hour flight carried them from Santiago to Easter Island. Woody had never seen a hotel like the Altiplanico. It was made up of a string of private buildings; theirs had a single room with a king-sized bed that faced two large glass sliding doors.

They had a spectacular view out across the island and into the ocean.

The plan was to stay for four days. They intended to explore the Ana Kai Tangata caves the first afternoon, then relax in the evening. They dined on fresh seafood a stone's throw from the ocean.

It was beautiful.

And sedate.

After four days of casual exploration, Woody missed the adrenaline rush from strenuous hikes in the mountains and camping under the stars. He also didn't enjoy the façade of privacy. Their one-room bungalow didn't offer sufficient distance from the others to fully enjoy themselves.

Easter Island was beautiful and fascinating, but more of ticking a box on their bucket list than a favorite destination. They spent one more night in Santiago, eating their weight in hot dogs again, being driven around trying all the best restaurants and street vendors. *A salchicha tour.* He regretted the decision the following morning while tightening his belt on their flight to La Paz, Bolivia.

The Stannum Boutique Hotel and Spa would be their base camp for ten days. After the success of travelling in Peru, Estelle had booked a trekking guide for them. Juan Pablo had created an itinerary allowing them to hike multiple trails within driving distance of La Paz for ten days before heading farther into the country to visit the famous salt flats.

Estelle had also reserved a day at the spa for them. *What are we going to do at a spa? I always thought she had a sadistic streak in her.*

"Are these edible?"

"Cucumber?" Eddie lifted one off his eye to stare at Woody. "Did you just ask me if a vegetable was edible? I'll have Mama pray for you."

"They might put cream on them. For relaxing. How would I know what spa people do?" Woody popped the one from his left eye into his mouth. It tasted fine. "What the hell are we doing? We've got stinky mud caked on our faces and cucumber slices on our eyes. Why am I paying for this?"

"Relaxing." Eddie replaced the cucumber slice on his face. "Do you feel calm?"

"Hungry. I could eat a horse. Maybe not a horse." Woody tossed the other slice into his mouth. "We did a hot dog tour. How about an empada one here in La Paz?"

"Empada? You mean empanada?" Eddie snickered at him. "Think they call them salteñas here."

"Saltanas."

"Salteñas," Eddie repeated the word several times. "Bless your heart. You mean well."

"Bless yours right out the door." Woody sat up and picked at the dried clay on his face. "Next time Essie suggests a spa day, we'll roll around in the dirt outside and save time. Mud shouldn't be clean."

"There are better things to do in the mud." Eddie grinned, and Woody was immediately reminded of one of their nights camping in Seward. "Let's get out of here."

They made their way to the bathing cubicles attached to the spa. Woody glanced around the empty room. He grabbed Eddie by the arm to drag him toward one of the showers, slipping around the curtain and pulling it taut across the opening.

With a shared mischievous grin that cracked their mud masks, they tossed the towels around their waists over the top of the curtain rod. Woody backed up against the cold tile, allowing the warm water to cascade over him. Eddie followed him across the small space, crowding him underneath the shower.

Water obscured Woody's vision. He had to tilt his head to keep breathing. Their fingers expertly explored each other's bodies, already having learned all the pleasurably sensitive triggers along their skin.

Breathing heavy and hard, Woody reached down to wrap his hand around both of their shafts. Eddie thrust against him. Their dicks, slick with water and soap, glided together, with his fingers adding to the overwhelming sensations.

They tried to keep as quiet as possible. Eddie mouthed along his neck. Woody could feel him muffling his moans against his skin.

Their bodies rocked together, building up to a frenzy. Woody pressed his lips hard together when Eddie's teeth found the spot at the base of his neck that always sent an electric current through him direct to his shaft. His fingers tightened at the familiar sensation of going out of control.

"Damn." Woody leaned forward against Eddie to keep on his feet. The evidence of their pleasure disappeared down the drain, mixed with mud and warm water. "Now I really am starving."

"Well, at least we got a happy ending."

"I feel relaxed." Woody snickered. "Shower sex in a public locker room shower: check."

"Was that really on your list?"

"It is now." Woody grinned at him.

"You're nasty."

"And?"

"I love it." Eddie winked at him.

CHAPTER SIXTEEN

Juan Pablo, their guide to hiking around La Paz, had proven to be almost as organized as Estelle. The next week and a half had been planned out down to the hour. Their first official "on the itinerary" day involved exploring the city itself and Moon Valley.

Also, food.

Their guide to all things Bolivia had learned quickly how high exploring local cuisine was on their to-do list. Though, Juan Pablo hadn't quite understood Woody's joke about being growing boys. Some things, particularly colloquial phrases, didn't translate well.

Despite November being the warmest time of the year for La Paz, they'd found the temperature to be mild, even fairly cold in the evening. It had dipped down into the thirties their first night. Eddie was glad Estelle had insisted on them packing their clothes in layers.

"Didn't they call this Moon Valley?" Woody leaned over to whisper. They were standing at Devil's Point, looking across a canyon of rock formations that reminded Woody of something straight out of a sci-fi movie. "Shouldn't a *valley* be more… valley-like?"

"Less valley, more sandstone monuments created by wind and rain."

Woody nudged him with his elbow. "Sent a photo to Kat to share with my nieces. DeeDee apparently thinks we don't know how to make sandcastles."

"We don't."

Even with taking the longer of the two trails, they wrapped up their exploration of the strange wind-and-rain-created sandstone sculptures in the Valle de la Luna faster than expected. Juan Pablo showed yet again his understanding of them. He shortened their day out and took visiting the local museums off the itinerary.

Forgoing the museums and churches that usually made the list for the tour company, Juan Pablo brought them back to La Paz for something more exciting—cervezas and street food. They joined a few of his friends. The more, the merrier. The evening was perfectly mild for wandering around the city.

Bolivians had turned street food into an art. Eddie couldn't believe the sheer number of vendors who worked late into the night. Morning and evening seemed to be all about snacking on the go.

"Happy?" Eddie couldn't help laughing at Woody, who had six kebab skewers, three in each hand. They'd found a vendor who made *anticuchos*—a local delicacy. "You know that's grilled cow heart, right?"

"And?"

Eddie reached out to wipe the spicy peanut sauce

from Woody's chin. If they'd been alone, he would've licked it off. "How's the heart?"

"Juicy."

The *anticuchos* were surprisingly succulent and delicious. They'd continued with their goal to try local dishes without preconceived thoughts. Eddie managed to steal a second kebab from Woody, who'd tried to fight him off with a skewer.

They'd fought with skewers all the way down the street to the next vendor.

They ate their way through *chola* sandwiches (roast pork with chorizo), salty french fries covered with fried sausage and melted cheese, and deep-fried mashed potato balls. Eddie stopped keeping track of the beers—and the food. He wasn't even sure how they managed to walk back to their hotel without falling over.

He didn't remember getting to their room, getting naked, or falling asleep.

A ringing phone jolted Eddie awake before sunrise. He hadn't slept on a hard floor in years and definitely regretted all of his life choices. The obnoxious sound stopped as the front desk clearly gave up trying to wake them.

Rolling over on his side, Eddie spent a good two minutes staring at the hickeys on Woody's back—in the shape of a dick and balls. *Maybe if I don't mention it, he'll never notice. How long do love bites last? Gotta get a photo of this.*

Eddie reached out to fish his phone out of his jeans pocket and got proof of his masterpiece. He shook Woody's arm. "You up?"

"I'm something. We're too damn old to fall asleep on

the floor after a night of drinking and sex." Woody rolled over on his back. "Why're we up before the sun?"

"Hiking. The Cordillera Real. Sausage. Eggs." *And I hickey-tattooed a dick on your back.*

"Blowjobs?"

"Not on the itinerary. I checked. We'll make our own to-do list." Eddie got to his feet, stumbled over Woody's shoes, and moved forward to gather up his clothes. "We've got maybe ten minutes to get dressed before Juan Pablo shows up."

"Fuck."

Coffee and *buñuelos* set their day off better than waking up on the floor had. They ate a disturbingly large number of the deep-fried donut fritters. Eddie preferred the cheese-filled ones, while Woody hoarded the ones dripping with honey.

Today was the start of their five-day trek around the Cordillera Real. Juan Pablo had agreed to skip the day exploring an archaeological site an hour from La Paz. They were far more excited about hiking and camping in the mountains.

Backpacks. Gear. Guides. And an unnecessary second round of coffee and donuts. The perfect (and greasy) start to their next adventure.

Day three of their hike had so far been his favorite. Despite the high altitude and difficulty of the terrain, the views across the Bolivian Andes were spectacular. With shorter walking times than their treks in Peru, they had more time to explore each camping site.

Camping at Laguna Juri Khota offered a magical backdrop to their tents. They sat barefoot by the water, enjoying the bright sun overhead. The longer days gave them even more time to relax or clamber around the Andes.

Estelle had done a magnificent job of planning their trip, so they hiked increasingly difficult terrain across the year. They might not manage Everest by the end, but Eddie knew Woody hoped they could explore the base camp at least. Kilimanjaro was high on his list of mountains to summit.

Nights by the fire staring up at the stars had become one of Eddie's greatest joys. He leaned back against Woody, listening to the wood crackling nearby. Life had definitely managed to take an amazing turn for them.

Life at home hadn't sucked. But Eddie hadn't realized how much stress he'd been under. Now, in the mountains, resting against his best friend and lover, he noticed for the first time how much tension had gone from his body.

The following morning rain began to drizzle down on them. Better than a monsoon, but it made clambering over rocks complicated. Eddie made good use of their hiking sticks.

And then stumbled, skidded, and fell face-first up the trail.

"Shut. Your. Pie. Hole," Eddie grunted through gritted teeth at the snickering Woody who was out of sight. He lay flat on the ground, trying to catch his breath and assess the damage. "If you don't quit laughing, I'm shoving you off the mountain."

"Hard to do when you're face-first in the dirt."

Woody crouched beside his head. "You all right? Want a hand up?"

"Damaged pride." Eddie didn't think he'd broken or strained anything. He'd definitely bashed his knees and hands on the way down. "A few bruises and scrapes."

"I can think of better ways to bruise your knees."

"Kiss my grass." Eddie climbed to his feet, putting a hand on Woody's shoulder for stability. "Let's not do that again."

After two hours of limping, Eddie had never been so glad to see a parking lot. They climbed into the tour company's SUV. He was sad to say goodbye to the Cordillera Real and Juan Pablo but excited for the next stop on their Bolivian journey.

A night in the fancy hotel allowed him to soak in the Jacuzzi tub. Eddie's knees hurt a bit, and his hands stung from being scraped. He hoped it wouldn't be a problem on their next hike.

The following morning they flew partway, then drove to Salar de Uyuni—the famous Bolivian salt flats. They'd always fascinated Eddie. He'd seen the other-worldly images from people who'd gone and couldn't wait to screw around with Woody and their cameras.

How early do we have to get up to take naked photos on the salt flats?

We could use perspective to make our dicks look massive.

Priorities.

CHAPTER SEVENTEEN

WOODY

The salt flats were flat. And salty. And rainy. On the drive out to Uyuni clouds had begun to gather, and Woody wondered if their unnaturally good weather luck on the journey had finally run out.

It had.

Rain fell torrentially at times. They went from concerns about the perfect image to worrying about flash floods, mudslides, and getting stuck with no road access to the nearest city. The monsoon season had officially struck Bolivia.

If we were in Spain, I would be completely prepared for this thanks to Typing 101 in high school. The rains in Spain fall mainly on the plain. The most useless sentence finally comes in handy.

The view from their room meant nothing when ominous clouds obscured the sky twenty-four seven. They teased Estelle about not planning the weather to perfection. She suggested they play nice or she'd make their plane reservations accidentally vanish.

Mud.

Rain.

Boring.

Deciding not to risk a lengthy unintended stay, they left two days ahead of schedule. The weather in Uruguay, their next stop, wasn't much different. But they didn't intend to hike or stargaze.

They planned to spend most of their time enjoying thermal baths and the nightlife in Montevideo. Woody had talked Eddie into forgoing hikes for a few weeks. They'd be flying back home for the holidays, and he had a sneaking suspicion they'd be grateful for the chance to rest.

There would be drama at home. Estelle hadn't come right out and said it, but there'd been mixed reactions to their gifting of money to family. Woody knew his parents would be outraged at *not* getting what they believed was their due.

JJ hadn't waited for them to come home. He'd sent a barrage of texts to Woody a few days earlier. Then Kat had taken his phone from him—according to her message.

Christmas is going to be so much fun.

"Careful. You think too hard, you might break something." Eddie stepped up behind him. He rested his chin on Woody's shoulder, wrapping his arms around him. They stared out across Brava Beach from their penthouse suite at The Grand Hotel Punta Del Este. They had a sweeping view across the ocean. "You'll have steam comin' out your ears."

"Money."

"We're rolling in it."

Woody chuckled with Eddie for a second. "Have you heard anything from your folks about the money you've set aside for them?"

"Radio silence."

"Your family? Being silent?" Woody hadn't known they were capable of staying quiet on any subject for more than a day. "Maybe we should hang out in Uruguay for an extra week? Or the rest of our lives?"

"If you don't think my mama would track us down, you are completely mistaken." Eddie dragged him away from the window. "We have an hour before our dinner reservations and plenty of chairs to bend you over."

"My turn?" Woody muttered against Eddie's lips.

Their clothes were already strewn across the floor in a trail leading around the room from their exploring each other and the penthouse. Woody stumbled trying to kick off his boxers that he'd only pulled on ten minutes earlier. They went flying and landed on a vase, almost knocking it over. His laughter caught in his throat when he saw raw hunger in Eddie's eyes.

Eddie naked was a sight to behold—one Woody didn't think he'd ever grow tired of seeing. He'd been lusting after him since high school. His reminiscing flew right out of his mind when strong hands grabbed him by the hips, shoving him toward one of the chairs around the small dining table on the left of the room.

Despite the coolness of their suite, Woody felt nothing but warmth as Eddie leaned over him. He shivered when Eddie licked along his neck. His fingers ran down his back, caressing the sensitive skin at the base of his spine.

They'd already enjoyed the bed and the couch. Eddie slid into him easily. Woody ground back against him when Eddie's nimble fingers reached around to casually stroke his shaft.

Shifting to keep the edge of the chair from digging into his stomach, Woody pushed back, then forward, driving himself between Eddie's fingers and dick. No matter how many times Eddie filled him, Woody felt the same jolt of pleasure and overwhelming sexual joy.

Better with each new moment.

"How many times are you going to fall apart for me?" Eddie murmured into his ear, giving his shaft a hard stroke.

"Too many times for us to count. Just as many as you will for me." Woody groaned when Eddie pushed deeper into him. "*Fuck.*"

Ten minutes later, sprawled on the floor under the table with the chairs turned over, Woody made a mental note to leave a large tip for housekeeping. *And clean up a little with a towel. No need to traumatize anyone.*

We're thoughtful southern boys.

"I don't want to know why you're lying there snickering." Eddie sat up slowly. He pushed one of the chairs off his legs. "At least we didn't break anything."

Woody glanced behind him at the shattered vase. "You spoke too soon."

"Hide it under the couch."

"If that didn't work for Mama Ester when we broke her tea pitcher, I'm pretty sure the hotel staff will know we broke their expensive flower thing." Woody shifted carefully away from the sharp pieces. "Maybe we can glue it?"

"With the crazy glue you carry around in your back pocket?" Eddie stood up and stepped cautiously away from the area of the vase. "We'll confess our sins and offer to pay for the damage."

"Maybe don't mention how it broke."

"They'll probably guess." Woody paused before continuing. "You're a screamer."

"Kiss my grass." Eddie grabbed Woody's jeans and tossed them over to him. "Get dressed."

The concierge was very understanding. Woody could clearly hear her laughing when she went out of sight, supposedly to speak with housekeeping about cleaning up for them. She was wiping tears from her eyes when she returned. *Is this how millionaires live? Paying their way through embarrassing situations?*

Probably.

They made their dinner reservations with a few minutes to spare. Woody figured they didn't need to worry. Eddie, growing up around restaurateurs, had strict rules about not making life difficult for anyone who worked at a restaurant, no matter the size or number of stars.

Since joining the Facebook group for LPU, they'd gotten suggestions for places to visit and eat on every step of their journey. One couple who had been to Montevideo a month before suggested Garcia, a pricey-but-worth-it upscale restaurant. *You have to try the cocktails.* Woody had snickered for five minutes before

Eddie took his phone away and refused to let him respond.

"What exactly do you think makes the squid Roman?" Eddie asked. He pointed to the English description of one of the appetizers—Calamares a la Romana. "Do they have togas?"

Neither of them wanted to ask the waiter, so they ordered the appetizer to try it. They ordered several other appetizers that didn't sound like a friend of SpongeBob. On the suggestion of the server, they went with the fish paella and a rack of lamb.

It turned out to be the best paella he'd ever had.

Also, the only paella he'd ever had.

Over the course of the next few weeks, the two visited every thermal bath or hot spring within an easy drive from Montevideo. They lounged at the beach, ate their way through a long list of recommended restaurants, and enjoyed nights out on the active local gay scene. They also argued about whether hand jobs in the bubbling water went against common courtesy.

They never could decide but had a lot of fun and were sorry to say goodbye to Uruguay when it came time to return to South Carolina for Christmas. Their families were expecting them. Estelle had warned them she'd heard grumblings about their decision to gift money.

As a result, they'd switched their flight to land early. Woody didn't agree with Eddie's assessment that it would let them have a moment to relax. The Howards were definitely *not* about to be subtle about their opinions.

They'd be kind, but not subtle.

"It's an ambush." Woody stared through the windshield at the serious faces lined up in front of Eddie's house. "Estelle didn't mention a welcome committee."

"Is it too late to drive back to the airport? Iceland is calling." Eddie took a sip of coffee; they'd stopped for donuts and java for a boost of energy before getting off the interstate. "Maybe they'll go away?"

"Your folks? Randomly go away?"

"Shut your pie hole," Eddie muttered. "C'mon. Mama will hug the truck if we don't get out and face the music."

"Y'all getting out?" Carlton glanced between his son and Woody.

"Let's go." Woody slid out of the vehicle and waited for the inevitable.

Hugs happened. Mama Howard's embraces always reminded Woody of a rich berry cobbler in the middle of winter—warm, sweet, and comforting. Nothing like his own mom, who was more like being shoved into an ice bath.

"We goin' inside?" Carlton draped his arm across his son's broad shoulders. "We brought food. We'll have a little sit down. Enjoy food and talk."

Shit.

"I should check in on JJ, make sure he hasn't fallen off a ladder or cut his arm off with a buzz saw." Woody tried unsuccessfully to edge away from the front door. Mama Ester blocked his escape route. She caught his hand in hers, pulling him forward. "Or I could wait."

"Your people are coming over for supper," she assured him. "Kat's bringing her peach cobbler."

"Great." Woody exchanged a resigned look with Eddie. Time had definitely come to face the response for their leaving money in trusts for their family. "Can't wait."

The biggest room in Eddie's place was the dining room. He'd been gifted a large, antique table by his parents when he'd moved into his home. It had enough space to fit all of them plus JJ and Kat if the girls were at their grandparents.

Food and family. The two elements always mingled at the Howard house. Mama Ester claimed the spice came from her side while the soul came from her son-in-law's people. Woody had always envied the generous spirit of love in their home.

Halfway through the meal, Carlton pointed his fork at Eddie and demanded to know why their wishes had been ignored. All of their wishes. They hadn't wanted money.

Eddie set his own fork down, took a long sip of his iced tea, and glanced briefly over at Woody. "Pretend you won the Publisher's Clearinghouse and you're gonna get a check every month for the rest of your life."

"Eddison." Edna shook her head at her son.

Woody reached down to take his hand in an offer of support. He could see JJ was itching to make comments of his own. "We were never going to *not* share the wealth. My dumb luck was too good not to spread around."

"We don't need—"

"Who does?" Eddie stood up quickly, cutting off his dad. "Who actually needs so much money they can never spend even a quarter of the winnings? If you're so bothered, donate all of it. Lord love a duck."

Woody watched Eddie storm out of the room, and they heard the back door slam shut a moment later. "If y'all would excuse me."

"Stay." Carlton got up and followed his son.

Woody turned his attention to his brother, who sat across the table from him. "How about you?"

JJ opened his mouth, then seemed to reconsider after Kat elbowed him. "Suppose you won't change your mind no matter what I say."

"Suppose you're right." Woody nodded with a wry grin at JJ.

"Right, but don't you dare buy me a present ever again." JJ saluted him with his glass of iced tea.

"When did I ever buy you a present?"

"Cheap…. Guess I can't call you a cheap son of a gun anymore." JJ laughed along with him. He grunted when Kat elbowed him again. "What I meant to say was, thanks, brother."

CHAPTER EIGHTEEN

EDDIE

EDDIE STARED ACROSS HIS BACKYARD. HIS COUSINS HAD done a good job keeping up with the falling leaves while he'd been traveling. They'd even stocked up his wood-pile along the fence for the winter. "Not saying sorry for helping my family."

His dad stepped up beside him with his hands shoved in his pockets. "Stubborn as a mule. You get it from your mama's side. They're all hardheaded, just like you."

Eddie rolled his eyes. His dad liked to pretend he was easygoing when, in reality, stubbornness ran on both sides of their family. "Still not saying sorry."

"Of course, you aren't. And if you did, I know you'd be lying through your teeth." He pulled a hand out of his pocket and rubbed the back of his neck absently. "Your mama says I've got too much Howard pride in my veins."

"Think they call that being stubborn."

"Your sass is unappreciated." His dad managed a

scowl for a second before smiling at him. "That's from your mama's side."

"Do you two ever get tired of blaming each other for my negative traits?"

"If you ever have kids, you'll understand why we'll never grow tired of complaining and embarrassing you. It makes up for all the times you peed in my face while I changed your diapers." He threw his arm around Eddie's shoulders. "We're proud of you."

Eddie grimaced at the millionth mention of the diaper changing escapades of his infancy. "Proud I stumbled into money?"

"Proud of your generous spirit." His dad squeezed his shoulders tightly. "And you never listen."

"I listened."

"You never listen."

Eddie considered for a moment, since his dad had a point. He'd spent most of his teen years making impulsive decisions that frequently veered far off his parents' advice. "Gonna be a cold winter."

"It is." His dad twisted toward Eddie and tugged him into a tight hug. "And I'm gonna let you change the subject because your mama might make me sleep on the couch."

Eddie patted his dad on the back and stepped back. He returned to watching the sunset. "Thinking about asking Woody to marry me."

Silence.

His dad cleared his throat a few times. "Prepare yourself for the Howard women taking over the planning. And for his folks going even further off the deep end. They mean well, God love them."

"They don't mean well. And I'm sure they believe their god loves them and their hatred," Eddie said sharply. "Sorry. How can they treat their own blood like dirt yet also want to use him as a damned money machine?"

"No accounting for some people." He shoved his hands into his pockets again. "We should go inside before we freeze. When are you going to propose?"

"Christmas? Or maybe on our next hike." Eddie hadn't thought much about the how of proposing. "We could elope."

"Do you want your mama and grandma to skin you alive?"

"So, no eloping." Eddie wondered if Estelle might help with his idea. She had a way of making the impossible happen, even with a short timeframe to create miracles. "We better head inside before they send out a search party."

"Tell your mama I was nice."

They spent the rest of their evening sharing stories about traveling. Woody had brought along snacks purchased from various locations. They'd been careful to pick chips and candy that customs allowed into the country; they'd spent an hour reading through the ins and outs of what wouldn't get them in trouble.

Except for the banana Eddie had snuck into Woody's backpack. It had been an expensive prank. The customs agent at the airport hadn't been as amused as Eddie.

They'd waited until they were safely out of the airport before cracking up laughing. Eddie had spent most of the drive home making "is that a banana in your pocket?" jokes. It had definitely been worth the fine for bringing in a piece of fruit.

And it had not been a banana in Woody's jeans.

Not on the way back from the airport.

One of these days we're going to get pulled over.

Woody

"Really?" Woody was confused by the gift in his hand. He'd lifted the lid of the silver box with his name on it and found a scratch-off lottery card. "Thanks."

Eddie tossed a quarter at him. "You never know. You might win another million."

Woody frowned at the quarter, then at the card. "But—"

"Just try it," Eddie grumbled.

I know it's the thought that counts, but a lottery card? Really?

Deciding to humor Eddie, Woody used the edge of the quarter to rub against the first gray circle. He frowned at the 'M' revealed underneath. *What the hell?* Eddie refused to look at him and seemed incredibly focused on an already opened present.

"Ed?"

Nothing.

With a confused shake of his head, Woody returned

to the card in his hand. His fingers and the quarter were covered in gray dust when he finished. *Marry me? What kind of lottery is this? Did I win?*

Marry me?

What?

Oh. Marry me?

Woody snapped his head up to stare at Eddie while still trying to process. "Marry me?"

"Well?"

"Marry me?" Woody wondered if his brain had short-circuited. He was struggling to make sense of what was happening. "Marry me?"

"It's legal." Eddie tapped his fingers against the box in his hands.

"Marry *me?*" He waved the lottery card around wildly.

"If you say it one more time without actually answering me…." Eddie didn't finish his threat. Woody couldn't recall ever seeing him so nervous. "Well?"

"Marry you?"

"I swear you were smarter than this an hour ago. Should I change my mind?" Eddie crushed the empty box in his hand and tossed it aside. He glared when Woody started to laugh at him. "Linwood Robinson."

"Yes?" Woody tried to sound calm and collected, but the word came out as squeaky and more question than statement. He cleared his throat, rolling his eyes in aggravation when it was Eddie's turn to laugh at him. "You really want to get married?"

"The interest is starting to fade."

Woody dove across the room, tackling Eddie and

taking him and the chair backward to the floor. "We're getting married."

"Did your brain finally kick back into gear?" Eddie rolled off the edge of the chair. He dragged Woody with him, looming over him with their lips almost touching. "We can run off to the courthouse."

"If we elope, your mama will hunt us down and skin us alive. So, no, we're not eloping." Woody had no doubt the Howard women would want to make an event out of it—no matter what their thoughts on the subject were. "Is that a candy cane in your pocket, or are you happy to see me?"

"Why don't you give it a lick and find out?" Eddie twisted his body around practically shoving his groin into Woody face. "Oh look, there's one in your trousers as well."

"Dumbass."

Reaching out, Woody pulled down the waistband on Eddie's boxers and sweatpants. His fingers danced along the shaft of Eddie's already semihard erection. *Merry, merry Christmas morning to us.*

"Never had one of these in my Christmas stocking before." Eddie teased him with words and skilled fingers tracing around the head of his dick. "Always so eager."

"I'm a growing boy." Woody chuckled before dragging his tongue along Eddie's warm flesh. "So are you."

Eager definitely described him every single time Eddie's velvety soft, dark skin was exposed. Months of intimacy after years of nothing but watching from afar hadn't diminished their enthusiasm for each other. They were starving men who'd learned never to take love and lust for granted ever again.

Woody found himself thinking back to some of the lonely nights when he'd wondered if his dreams would ever come true. He buried them so deeply inside. "I love you."

Eddie pulled back from his pleasurable ministrations to meet Woody's gaze. "Because I'm licking your dick?"

"Don't be an ass." Woody flicked him on the inner thigh. "Marriage. Love. Blowjobs on Christmas morning. A year ago, I woke up on my own and wondered if I was ever going to have the courage to ask you out."

"And you want to have this conversation now?" Eddie glanced down at the hard shaft in his hand. "Right now?"

"It can wait."

There were only two words to describe their version of sixty-nine. *Competitive blowjobs.* Woody didn't see the point in taking his time, and neither did Eddie. They dove into the challenge of getting one another off with a vengeance.

The unspoken goal was always to see who could make the other lose control first. In the travel journal Eddie kept, Woody knew a section had been dedicated to keeping score. They were currently tied.

Not for long.

I'm going ahead this morning—pun intended.

Flicking his tongue along the underside of Eddie's shaft, Woody smiled against the warm flesh when it throbbed against him. He grabbed Eddie's balls, squeezing lightly before tugging on them. With his lips wrapped around him, Woody began to move up and down.

He wanted Eddie to completely lose his ability to focus. Hard to manage with the talented lips working his own dick. *We're both winners, right? Definitely. Concentrate. Pretend we're in the last five minutes of a game and the entire season depends on you catching the ball.*

Or, balls.

And the bat, wait that's not football.

Not focusing.

Holy fuck.

What's he doing with his tongue?

He didn't win.

He came a close second.

CHAPTER NINETEEN

EDDIE

Christmas had gone as well as expected. They'd spoiled their family with presents for the first time in their lives. The day after, Eddie had asked his parents to distract Woody while he took care of business.

Taking JJ and their old high school buddy turned attorney, Judge, along for the ride, Eddie had met up with Woody and JJ's parents outside of their church. He'd wanted them to feel the illusion of being on their own turf.

"A hundred thousand dollars." Eddie didn't waste time on small talk once they'd gathered outside in the parking lot. He'd refused the offer to go inside and sit down. "A hundred thousand, and you leave us alone. Forever. Take it or leave it."

"We're not—"

"Who are you talking to? Not me. I've known you most of my life. Don't even try." Eddie had no intention of listening to any feigned piety. "A hundred thousand.

You leave Woody alone. You quit your lying about him around town. You don't even whisper his name."

"How dare you." Mrs. Robinson would've clutched her pearls if she'd been wearing them.

Eddie glared at her in silence until she closed her mouth. Her fake offense didn't affect him at all; neither did her crocodile tears. "This isn't a difficult concept. Bless your simple little hearts. What's it going to be?"

"Five hundred thousand." Mr. Robinson wrapped an arm around his wife's shoulders and drew her back. They all ignored the sharp gasp from JJ, who stood off to the left with Judge. "And we'll leave you to the devil."

Eddie didn't know why JJ was surprised by his parents. They'd written their oldest son off the moment he came out of the closet. "Two hundred. Not a penny more. Judge wrote up a legal document with the details. You sign it. He'll get the money transferred wherever you want it. You break your word, and I'll do my very best to destroy you completely."

"He's your son." JJ had always tried to walk the fine line between his parents and his brother. Eddie knew the youngest Robinson brother had held out hope of some sort of reconciliation. "Your flesh and blood. And he's gay and in love with this dumbass over here. I done read the Bible you preach from cover to cover. Nowhere in there does it say to throw your children away because they've fallen in love with someone. It says judge not lest ye be judged, doesn't it? You make me sick. If you take this money, and I know you will, don't come onto my property. I'll call the sheriff on you."

"C'mon, man." Eddie wrapped his arm around JJ's

shoulders to lead him away from his parents. He'd planned to go with only Judge, but JJ had shown up while they'd been planning and insisted on going with them. "I'm sorry."

"Why?" JJ shook his head at him. "What am I going to tell my girls? At least they have Kat's parents."

"And my folks. You know my mama and daddy love them to pieces. You've got family, JJ." Eddie had known the Robinsons would take the money. Their avarice had always hovered beneath the surface. "Why don't you head home and bring your girls and Kat over to my parents' place? We're having leftovers and watching movies most of the day."

After JJ drove off, Eddie leaned against his truck and watched Judge iron out the details with the greedy reverend. He was disgusted at the lack of hesitancy on their part as they signed the documents. They'd placed such little value on their children and grandchildren. *Is a relationship worth two hundred thousand dollars?*

The pettiest part of him felt some satisfaction in knowing the legal agreement wouldn't stay a secret. Nothing stayed completely hidden in a small town like theirs. He'd seen several people driving by slowly and had no doubt rumors had already started flying.

A small but satisfying consolation.

Eddie arrived back at Woody's place an hour later after finishing up with Judge. He found Woody drinking coffee in the backyard next to the fire pit. "Morning. Had breakfast yet?"

"Waited for you. How were my folks?"

Lord love a duck.

Mothertrucker.

"Woody."

"Did they accept whatever you and Judge managed to put together?" Woody sipped his coffee slowly, still staring at the roaring fire. "JJ called me when he left. He's handling this better than I thought. Think he always held out hope they'd suddenly become the decent, God-fearing Christians they always claimed to be."

"I'm...." Eddie trailed off. He wasn't sorry, not even a little. "You all right?"

"How much did it cost you?"

"Woody."

He glanced over at Eddie with a completely blank expression. "How much?"

"Two hundred big ones."

Woody took another drink from his mug. "They don't deserve a damn cent from us."

"My cent."

Woody glanced over the rim of the mug at him. "They abandoned me years ago. This only makes it official."

Eddie dragged one of the deck chairs over to sit next to him. He grabbed Woody's hand. "You all right?"

Woody shrugged.

"Mama's making breakfast for the family. JJ and all of them will be there as well." Eddie hated when Woody shut himself off. He'd learned how to do it far too well as a teenager. "Wood?"

He reclined back against the wooden chair, still

holding Eddie's hand. "Let's just sit by the fire, okay? Just the two of us."

Eddie stared at him for a second.

"And don't sing the damn song. You're not Will Smith."

"Mothertrucker." Eddie stretched out on the deck chair and grinned over at Woody. "I had an idea."

"Another one? How much is this one going to cost you?" Woody smiled, and the tightness in Eddie's chest dissipated.

"About this marriage thing."

"Yeah?"

"What if we rented a plane, flew everyone to Vegas, and got married there? Not eloping, but also technically not a wedding?" Eddie stole Woody's cup and finished his coffee. "Estelle already booked the flight for us."

"Any other life plans you've made for us?"

"The family is *not* coming on our honeymoon." He set the cup on the edge of the chair, leaned forward to grab Woody by the shirt, and leaned over him for a kiss. "I love you. Marry me?"

"Fine. But, no Elvis."

"Mothertrucker."

"We could be in Vegas, sitting by the pool, drinking beers with those umbrellas in them and enjoying the sun." Eddie stood next to Woody. They shivered by the edge of a cliff, looking down at a waterfall. "Why are we freezing in Iceland?"

"Your cousins kept winking at us whenever we came downstairs from our room for breakfast at the hotel." Woody had a feeling Estelle had booked them all into the same floor for the sole purpose of teasing her cousin. She had definitely done it on purpose. "Would you rather freeze or have another walk of shame while your dad is laughing at us?"

"Freeze."

"I've never agreed with a sentiment more." Woody rubbed his gloved hands together and turned his face away from the wind. "Though, in retrospect, we could've picked a better time to come to Iceland."

The wedding had been short, with no Elvis impersonator, much to JJ's disappointment. His brother had tried to sneak one into the ceremony. Estelle and Kat had made certain his prank didn't see the light of day.

His nieces had danced them down the aisle. Flower girls without the rose petals. They hadn't bothered with suits, and their reception had been at one of the largest buffets in Vegas.

Having their entire family in Vegas for their impromptu wedding had been great. And then they'd all stayed in the same hotel. On the same floor. He'd swear to his dying day that Estelle had planned it.

They'd been enjoying a slow morning in bed when Eddie's dad had pounded on the door. *Breakfast. Get your asses up.* Woody had quickly realized honeymoons should happen far away from family.

For their sake.

And for the sake of his erection.

Several of their friends from the gay hiking group had recommended traveling to Iceland in the off-peak season to avoid crowds. It did up the difficulty level on their hikes. They'd swapped out some of their gear to be better equipped to handle the frigid temperatures and slick, frozen landscape.

Estelle had taken pity on them. She'd already booked flights for them and had their gear brought up from South Carolina where they'd left it. They definitely owed her so much for all the time spent organizing their year of adventure.

Winter in Iceland was cold and snowy. And icy. It had seemed like the perfect first stop on the next leg of their great adventure.

Leaning against the wooden barrier on the overlook, Woody watched the wind whip up the snow along the cliff edge and the water cascading over the edge. It was the closest he'd ever been to a live-action snow globe. Magical. And cold. He'd definitely lost feeling in at least five of his toes.

Eddie took a few photos before giving up and putting his gloves back on. "Can we go defrost?"

They planned to explore the Golden Circle for the first week in Iceland.

And Woody still couldn't say golden circle without snickering for a good minute or two.

Hanging out in their rented vehicle to warm up, they waited for their tour guide to arrive. Estelle had booked a snowmobile adventure for them. Woody couldn't wait to go flying across a glacier. Eddie had taken a little convincing, mostly because the few times he'd gone on a four-wheeler had all ended in crashes.

"We're going to die."

Woody glanced over at Eddie, who was gripping on to the handles of the snowmobile for dear life. "Probably. Though I doubt it's going to be today."

"You're a dickhead."

"Pretty sure the guides are laughing at you." Woody grinned, then pulled his helmet back on when Eddie went to throw a snowball at him.

Thirty minutes into their flying across the snow, Eddie had changed his tune. The ice tunnels into the glacier were a completely different story. Woody didn't enjoy them either.

Glaciers felt like slow-moving ice monsters. Living,

breathing creatures. Woody spent the entire trek inside the tunnels convinced they were going to collapse on them. He'd never really enjoyed caves in the first place —even ones carved out by humans.

Atli and Dyri, the married couple who ran the snowmobile tour company, had invited them out for beers and food afterward. They'd enjoyed spending the afternoon together. They hopped into their vehicle and followed them into Reykjavík.

"Not enough beer in the world for me to eat ram testicles. Nope." Woody shoved the plate toward Eddie while Atli and Dyri laughed at him. "I don't care if it has been boiled and fermented."

"How about fermented fish?" Atli held out her plate toward him.

"Those are my options? Fermented fish or balls?" Woody didn't think either of them should be consumed. He caught the coin Eddie tossed to him. "Worst heads or tails *ever*."

"It's neither heads nor tails." Eddie lifted his plate, which had braised sheep's head. "Want to trade?"

On their journey so far, Woody had tried a number of questionable cuisines. He tried to keep an open mind. The congealed ram balls tested his nerves.

Despite the occasional queasy nature of the cuisine, they enjoyed their evening of testing foods and washing them down with beer. The Icelandic couple helped them plan out their itinerary for the next week. They intended to stay around Reykjavík for a week before moving on to a remote hotel for a few days.

In two weeks, they'd be flying south to Andorra for two days, then moving on to meet up with a group of hikers from LPU. Safety in numbers. They intended to make their way through Morocco, Mali, and finally Tanzania.

They'd be in Tanzania for a month, since Kilimanjaro had been on both of their bucket lists. Not the hardest mountain in the world to summit but not a walk in the park either. The hike itself would only take ten days, but there were other places to explore in the country.

Lengai Volcano was one of the more strenuous hikes on their list. They'd camp by Lake Natron before attempting the six-hour trek in the dark to see the sunrise. Woody couldn't wait; he'd learned how to fly a drone over Christmas in the hopes of getting better videos to send home to their family.

Tanzania would take them through February into March. And then they'd be flying to Nepal. As a group, they planned to trek to the Everest base camp.

None of them wanted to summit the mountain itself.

Stretched out on their king-sized bed in their blissfully warm Icelandic hotel room, Woody scanned over their travel schedule for the next three months. He couldn't wait to catch up with their friends from Alaska and eat something that wasn't balls.

"Have you thought about Everest?" Eddie dropped on the bed beside him. He tapped his fingers against the map of Nepal. "We could afford the permit. Hell, we could get one for the whole group."

"Not interested in risking my life." Woody had considered it briefly, but he'd watched so many movies and documentaries on Everest. He knew the dangers; even making it to base camp would stretch some of their group to the limit. "We just got married. Not ready to shove you off a mountain yet."

"Shut your pie hole."

"Did you take an insurance policy out and not tell me?" Woody tried to gauge the level of seriousness from Eddie. "Do you really want to attempt the full summit?"

"My mama would fly out to Nepal, climb the mountain, and drag my behind home with her fingers pinching my ear." Eddie flipped the page of their travel journal to the portion after Everest. They intended to country hop across Asia until they reached Guangzhou, China, where they'd leave their hiking group to fly to Japan. "What are you most excited about?"

Woody rolled over on his back with his head resting on a map. "You."

"What?"

"You." Woody tilted his head so he could meet Eddie's steady gaze. "I'm most excited about spending my life with you. Married. Traveling the world with new friends. Not half-living my life in a job that barely pays the bills and burying my feelings for my best friend."

"Love, adventure, and ram testicles."

"I love you too." Woody snickered. "Ready for our next adventure?"

"Hey, if we turned this into a reality show, what would they call it?" Eddie lifted one of their cameras. "We could become famous."

"Dumbasses win the lottery and travel the world?" Woody blocked the hand that reached out to shove him off the bed. "Fools on vacation?"

And what a beautiful fucking journey it's going to be.

The End

ACKNOWLEDGMENTS

A massive thank you to my brilliant betas who take my first draft and help me turn it into something legible. To Becky, Olivia, and all the fantastic people at Hot Tree. And also to my beloved hubby who keeps me from losing my mind while I'm stressing over word counts.

And, lastly, thank you, readers, for following me on my writing journey. I hope you love this fun story as much as I do.

ABOUT THE AUTHOR

Dahlia Donovan wrote her first romance series after a crazy dream about shifters and damsels in distress. She prefers irreverent humour and unconventional characters. An autistic and occasional hermit, her life wouldn't be complete without her husband and her massive collection of books and video games.

Don't miss out on new releases, exclusive giveaways and much more!

Newsletter: http://eepurl.com/Q0n0X

Facebook: https://www.facebook.com/dahliadonovan

Reader group: https://www.facebook.com/groups/1326515147425106/

Twitter: https://twitter.com/DahliaDonovan

Pinterest: https://www.pinterest.com/dahliadonovan/

Goodreads: www.goodreads.com/author/show/8184061.Dahlia_Donovan

Instagram: https://www.instagram.com/dahliadonovanauthor/

BookBub: https://www.bookbub.com/authors/dahlia-donovan

Website: http://dahliadonovan.com/

Patreon: https://www.patreon.com/dahliadonovan

Dahlia would love to hear from you directly, too. Please feel free to email her at dahlia@dahliadonovan.com.

ABOUT THE PUBLISHER

Hot Tree Publishing opened its doors in 2015 with an aspiration to bring quality fiction to the world of readers. With the initial focus on romance and a wide spread of romance subgenres, Hot Tree Publishing have since opened their first imprint, Tangled Tree Publishing, specializing in crime, mystery, suspense, and thriller.

Firmly seated in the industry as a leading editing provider to independent authors and small publishing houses, Hot Tree Publishing is the sister company to Hot Tree Editing, founded in 2012. Having established in-house editing and promotions, plus having a well-respected market presence, Hot Tree Publishing endeavours to be a leader in bringing quality stories to the world of readers.

Interested in discovering more amazing reads brought to you by Hot Tree Publishing? Head over to the website for information:

WWW.HOTTREEPUBLISHING.COM